CAPITOL KISSES

I0894402

CAPITOL KISSES

KATHRYN LEWIS

Montlake Romance

The characters and events portrayed in this book are fictitious. Any similarity to real persons, living or dead, is coincidental and not intended by the author.

Text copyright © 1988 by Kathryn Lewis
All rights reserved.
Printed in the United States of America.

No part of this book may be reproduced, or stored in a retrieval system, or transmitted in any form or by any means, electronic, mechanical, photocopying, recording, or otherwise, without express written permission of the publisher.

Published by Montlake Romance
P.O. Box 400818
Las Vegas, NV 89140

ISBN-13: 9781477837641
ISBN-10: 1477837647

For Henry

This title was previously published by Avalon Books; this version has been reproduced from the Avalon book archive files.

Chapter One

Jenny Foster sat on a weathered bench, craving the Sunday solitude she always sought inside the public gardens of Dumbarton Oaks. Here silence reigned, interrupted only by the call of a bird or rush of the wind. The bustling streets of Georgetown, just beyond the surrounding brick walls, were easily forgotten.

Jenny welcomed the fog thickening around her, like layers of unbleached muslin wrapping her into a cocoon and shielding her from the outside world that swarmed with ringing telephones, conflicting appointments and clients.

It was five years ago that Jenny's friend, Anna Pitta, suggested they join forces and become personal-image consultants in Washington, D.C. Anna, who was quite a bit older than Jenny, had contacted several people in the image-making field and had accumulated a lot of sound advice. With her kids grown, she was eager to pursue the idea she had been mulling over for years. She was a former fashion model, and had plenty of experience and know-how for such an endeavor. But most important of all, Anna had contacts.

Her husband, Joe, had risen high in the foreign service, and together they had lived all over the world. Anna had many duties to perform as the wife of an American representative. She knew protocol inside out, and how to get along with international diplomats, businessmen, academics, workmen, and servants. Her world was a fast-paced one like Washington, where initial contact was often the only contact, and the first impression was very important.

Initially, Jenny didn't believe she could possibly offer anything to Anna's venture. Her own self-image was too badly in need of repair for her to think otherwise. Vance Dryden, the man who had said he loved her, had wrecked her self-esteem. But Anna persisted. She pointed out the inner strength Jenny had used to escape and survive her relationship with Vance. She made Jenny see the good that came out of her disastrous courtship. Living in Vance's jet-set world had broadened her horizons. She had acquired the manners of his upper-crust class. Exposed to tasteful luxuries and masterpieces, Jenny had developed an eye for good design and shape and could quickly distinguish quality items from second rate imitations. Anna's efforts to convince Jenny to use the skills she had learned for her own betterment paid off, and they became a team.

Jenny had found she was cut out for this work. She had always been attracted to people, and had majored in psychology and communications in college. She had also taken a minor in political science, hoping to land a slot as a news commentator eventually. Then Vance came and swept her off her feet.

Now, instead of being in front of the camera, she was behind it, showing television newscasters how to speak slowly yet forcefully and to come across better on the screen. She helped them and others too. She showed politicians how to employ the right body language and give a firm handshake, lawyers how to relax under pressure, business executives how to look confident and to maintain eye contact, and professors how to dress for interviews. Jenny worked on her clients from head to toe, and when necessary called on psychologists, dance instructors, hair stylists, and other professionals for assistance. She did everything possible so her client would achieve that much-desired "style." It was this caring attention to all details that she and Anna gave that made the firm of Foster and Pitta so sought after.

But right now she was glad to be away from it all, and especially away from one of her clients, Steve Voight. He had walked in and done a good job of turning her life upside down.

Jenny had been attracted to Steve the first moment he entered her office. He was a farmer from the Midwest, and she guessed he had gotten his suit back there. The tailor had not done him justice—the brown polyester suit he wore didn't fit at all. His build was solid and firm, like the farm boys whose muscles grow with each lifted bale of hay and roped cow. Steve had pulled at the collar several times, obviously unaccustomed to wearing a tie. He belonged in dungarees and an open shirt, roaming free around his ranch. Jenny found his ruggedness a welcome change from the sophisticated but prissy men she knew.

Steve had come to Washington as a volunteer with a cattlemen's association. He had been an active member on the Young Cattlemen's Council back home. The recent drought had compounded the farmer's plight, and Washington's slow response infuriated Steve. The cattlemen's association was glad when he offered his help. It was a grass-roots organization, dependent on farmers like Steve who were willing to give freely of their time out of a sense of responsibility and dedication.

Steve had inherited his farm from his family, and without the debt other farmers had, had managed to be successful. He didn't have family and financial worries, and could afford to hire people to run his farm for the year he planned to spend in Washington. The cattlemen's association paid for his traveling expenses, but his living expenses came out of his own pocket.

He had told Jenny that he didn't want his year to end without the government doing something constructive for the farmer. And he was willing to take any measures necessary to ensure that he would be heard, even if that meant he had to pay her to change him from a hick farmer, as he called himself, into what he thought was a Washington sophisticate.

Steve was so easy to work with. His sense of humor was solid and spontaneous, not the string of jokes some of her other clients used to cover up their insecurities. Never once did she need to engage in a psychological battle with him. Nor did she need to break through a macho barrier, or tread around a fragile ego, or pep up a weak spirit. He could stand aside and look at himself objectively, and still feel comfortable about himself and why he wanted her to polish up his image. But the more Jenny worked with him the more she found herself wondering, *Why change him when he is so right the way he is?*

Her objectivity was clouding over in regard to Steve. And Jenny had begun to feel she could no longer be fair to him. She had suggested he consult Anna, giving the excuse that she was too busy to give him the attention he deserved. But he said he would wait, he was comfortable with her. But she wasn't very comfortable with him, not when the thought of him kept haunting her. She tried not to let her feelings show. She had trained herself to keep up her professional demeanor, no matter what, and hoped Steve would continue to think of her as nothing more than an image consultant—a hired hand.

As this drizzly, dreary March afternoon passed, the air became cooler, and Jenny drew her legs up under her trench coat for warmth. Her shoulder-length hair, as golden as newly harvested wheat, fell to one side as she rested her head on her knees and thought about Steve. Jenny Foster, at least the Jenny Foster she had made herself into, would never have dared to allow her fantasies to run free, especially when they involved being kissed by a client. She was supposed to be cool, elegant, and always in control. But how could she possibly continue working with Steve when he rattled her so?

The sound of footsteps startled Jenny. She looked up and turned in the direction of the sound. Through the fog, she spotted a blotch of red and was barely able to discern the figure of a tall man. Her eyes followed his red-and-black checked jacket as he meandered around a barren flower bed, his hands in his pockets. If he circled back, he would be coming her way. She kept her chin on her knees and looked straight ahead, but out of the corner of her eye she saw that he was no longer walking with his head down. He had turned back along the path leading to her alcove. He was looking at her. She looked up with a smile ready for the passing stranger. But the second he came close enough for her to recognize him, her heart started to pound. He called out her name, sounding unsure if she was really Jenny.

The heavy mist folded back as Steve Voight approached her. "Well, I'll be darned. I hardly recognized you," he said, giving her one of his smiles. He had the nicest, warmest, most natural smile she had ever seen. It always made her smile back.

"You caught me with my mask off," she said. "I didn't expect to run into anyone here on such a miserable day." *Least of all you,* she added to herself. Her heartbeat slowed as she gradually regained her composure.

Steve settled down next to her, sitting sideways in order to face her, and resting his arm over the back of the bench. Overhead, a mass of tangled, dead-looking wisteria branches that in several months would bloom into clusters of lavender flowers, covered a trellis. "Well, I'm sure glad I did. I never realized how pretty you are." He couldn't possibly mean that. She looked awful wearing old clothes and no makeup. She was surprised he had even recognized her. "Jenny, you don't think I'm joking, do you?"

"I'm not too sure. I'll have to take a look in the mirror when I get home."

"And look hard, because you're mighty pretty. Your eyes are as crystal blue as a mountain lake." He spoke objectively, without a trace of false flattery. "Funny, I never noticed that before."

"Enough about my eyes," Jenny said, amused that the eye shadow she usually wore hadn't worked for him. "What's brought you to Dumbarton Oaks?"

He was slow to answer, his dark eyes burrowing into hers. "I came to see the pre-Colombian art collection in the mansion, but I've found something better."

"You mean the gardens?" Jenny said, feeling faint under his gaze and knowing full well that wasn't what he meant.

His mouth twitched in a suppressed smile. "I haven't seen the gardens." Jenny wished her heart would stop racing. "Maybe you could show them to me."

Jenny tried to smile as she stood up, glad for a less-personal topic of conversation. They walked down a cobbled path. "Do you come here often?" Steve asked.

"Every Sunday I can get away."

"I can see bad weather doesn't stop you."

"I guess I'm addicted to this place. A few hours here, and I feel like I've been on a week's vacation."

He looked more in character in his dungarees than he did in a business suit, and just as good looking. Jenny thought of Enzio, the hair stylist she had sent Steve to. He was one of the best. Enzio would be having fits if he could see Steve's thick, dark hair now. He had meticulously shown Steve how to blow-dry his hair back in sweeping motions, giving him a polished, distinguished look. The settling mist had undone all that, or perhaps Steve hadn't bothered to blow-dry his hair. Regardless, Jenny found the loose, easy waves of Steve's hair much more appealing.

"Most people don't think there's much to see at the gardens this time of year," she said, feeling his eyes on her.

"But I know otherwise."

She looked up at him. Again his eyes told her he wasn't referring to the gardens. She turned away, afraid her eyes might betray her feelings for him. As they walked side by side, Jenny raised the collar of her coat, then put her hands into her pockets.

"Are you cold?" he asked.

"A little."

"We can leave if you like," Steve suggested.

"No, I'm fine."

He put his arm around her shoulders, keeping her close to his side. "Better?"

"Much," she said. She looked up over her shoulder at him. His eyes were already on her.

He nudged her closer, and she nestled her shoulder under his arm. They strolled across the terrace where great stone urns stood in the center of box-edged parterres. She felt the long fingers of his strong hand gently spread out over her shoulder, guiding her close as they walked, so not even a draft of cool air could pass between them. She worried how she was ever going to retain her professional demeanor with Steve when his arm was around her.

A lawn spread out before them, bordered with different shrubs, hollies, and tall, feathery pines, all deeply green. Jenny tried to concentrate on the view, wanting to avoid his eyes as much as she could. She understood nonverbal communication and body language well, and didn't want to convey the wrong message to him—a message she was unwilling to have him hear.

Turning back, they came to an area walled off from the rest of the garden. Inside was a zodiac circle inlaid on a flagstone patio. "When's your birthday?" he asked, walking around the symbols.

"April twenty-eighth."

"So, you're a Taurus."

"Are you interested in astrology?" she asked.

"Not much. I've read a bit on it, mostly because I'm fascinated that it has endured so long."

"What's your sign?"

He studied her for a moment, as if he wasn't sure he should tell her. "Scorpio," he said, waiting for her reaction.

"The most difficult sign in the zodiac."

"Don't let that scare you. I'm really a pussycat."

She had read enough to know this was true of Scorpios if you truly understood them. And if you did, according to the books, their love would be the kind most women dreamed of.

Since Vance, her contact with men had been mostly business. She had dated a little after she broke off her engagement to him, but as soon as any relationship showed signs of becoming serious, that old, anxious, panicky feeling would return. People had said she wasn't the marrying kind. They couldn't possibly have thought anything else when she left Vance. He was every woman's dream—charming, good-looking, and extremely wealthy. Only she knew the private misery she would have endured as Mrs. Dryden.

Falling in love was not for her. And she knew she'd be foolish to let Steve change her mind. *But how silly of me,* she thought, admonishing herself for having jumped to such conclusions. He had his arm around her, and already she was thinking he might want to marry her. He could be just trying to keep her warm. He was just being gentlemanly. And when he said her eyes were as crystal blue as a mountain lake—well, he was just making conversation. That was all. She was his hired hand, and for both their sakes, it was better it stayed that way.

Steve squeezed her shoulder and asked, "Is there any more to see?"

"Yes, there's the waterlily pond a little farther down."

Walking around the pond, he was silent while she rambled on about the different people who had lived in the mansion. She could feel him tensing and could see his jawbone tighten. This shouldn't be happening. She stood taller and accentuated even more her professional "New England" voice. They circled up along a winding path through boxwoods so tall that they almost formed a canopy. "There's really quite a history to Dumbarton Oaks. A treaty ending one of the wars was signed here."

"World War Two," he said, stopping short and facing her. "Jenny, relax. You're off duty."

She turned red, realizing that she had managed to master her feelings for him and had resumed playing her role. But that was what she was supposed to do: practice diction, posture, walk, and mannerisms—all modeled on an ideal image—until it became second nature. But here was Steve standing in front of her, making her realize that the New England voice she used was not her Midwestern twang, but the way Vance talked. Steve was forcing her to see beyond the mirror of her image, to see that the ideal she was trying to copy was Vance. So what if she had copied him? It had been her ticket to success.

And she was determined not to risk losing what she had worked so hard to achieve. Even if it meant not loving again. She was doing so well on her own. She'd never let herself go back to the insecure, frightened, farm girl she had once been.

With a gentle plea, Steve said, "Jenny, I was really enjoying finding you off duty. Can't it stay that way?"

"Once a business relationship is established, it's hard to change," she said firmly, trying to resist the tenderness in his voice and in his eyes.

Gently his fingers touched her chin and slowly lifted her face to his, making her look into his eyes. His eyes were mesmerizing as he bent closer to her. He smiled as he put his arms around her and drew her close. His lips were warm as they touched hers ever so lightly—just a gentle touch, like a warm summer breeze, then a reluctant parting. His eyes met hers. "I think it's just changed," he said with a smile, hugging her close.

Her mind told her she shouldn't let this happen. She should push him away, resume her professional stance. But then she felt the softness of his cheek brush against her forehead, and she was powerless. It felt so right to be in his arms.

"It's getting dark," he whispered into her ear.

Jenny looked at her watch. It was five o'clock. "Oh, no," she said. "They'll be closing the gates soon, and I wanted to show you the music room in the mansion."

"Let's save that for another time."

She knew she should be wary of another time with him, but couldn't help wanting to be with him again. Walking toward the main gate, he offered her his arm. As she took it, he clasped her hand in his, then slipped it into the warmth of his coat pocket. "Would you have dinner with me?" he asked. "That is, unless you have other plans."

"Oh, I wish I could, but I promised Anna I'd help her host a fund-raiser tonight. Hey, why don't you come? There will be so many people—one more won't make any difference."

"I think I'll pass. You'll be busy with the guests. Besides, I've been to enough of those parties. They're real zoos."

"I know what you mean. Can I take a rain check on dinner?"

"You bet."

Jenny opened the door of her battered, blue MGB and offered Steve a lift. It would be unwise for her to change her plans and stay with him, though she was tempted. Thank goodness Anna was depending on her tonight.

"Where's the black Mercedes you chauffeured me in to that custom tailor where I spent a small fortune on two suits?" Steve asked. Jenny knew the suits weren't expensive by Washington standards, but probably would be back home.

She smiled at the sight of his tall body hunched over in the seat of her sports car. "You're made for a Mercedes. The one I drove you in belongs to Anna. She lives out in Potomac, where the houses have lots of acreage, circular driveways, and three-to-four-car garages. Sometimes I think I should trade in my MGB for something nicer. But I don't have a garage, and I'd worry about it getting banged up on the street. This one has so many dents, another one wouldn't even show. And it gets me where I'm going." The car backfired and Steve laughed. "So far," she said, patting the dashboard.

The street lights were just turning on as she pulled into Dupont Circle. Lines were forming for movies; restaurant doors were swinging open. Couples were everywhere, and she and Steve were saying good-bye.

"Thanks for the ride," he said with a wink. "I think I'll be spending enough time in Washington to be thinking about getting a car of my own." He leaned over to her. He gave her a quiet kiss, nothing more. "See you soon," he said, waving to her as he walked away. She wanted to feel his arms around her again and his lips on hers, but part of her was afraid.

Jenny knew that Steve and her other clients would never have guessed that one of her most successful image remakes had been her own. None of them knew the last-ditch effort she had made to salvage her badly damaged ego, and the struggle that ensued to get where she was. But that was five years ago and centuries away, it seemed, from the young girl who once ran barefoot through cornfields. It was something she didn't like to dwell on. But it was something that left her sympathetic to any feelings of inferiority her clients might have, and the awkwardness of their needing her help to improve themselves.

Jenny thought how little she knew about Steve—just that he was involved with the farming bill and was very busy pushing it into legislation. She did know, however, that every time he walked into her office his smile would warm her through and through. But she had a feeling that even a squirrel in a park would get the same smile, and certainly every girl who came his way. Steve was so open, so in love with the world. But today his smile had been only for her, and she had found herself liking it.

* * *

"Hetty, I'm home," Jenny said, flinging open the large panel door of an expensive, prewar townhouse near Kalorama Circle. Amber, Hetty's calico cat, ran up to greet her, her tail erect in salute. Jenny took off her trench coat and shook her hair free. Then she lifted Amber close to her and cradled the purring cat under her chin.

"Hi, love," Hetty called from the library. Hetty, a grandame in her eighties, was Jenny's landlady and closest friend. It was through her that Jenny had met Anna Pitta.

Jenny walked back to the library, carrying Amber in her arms. Hetty was arranging glasses on a silver tray. "I'm not going to have time for cocktails tonight," Jenny said. "I have to get over to Anna's."

Hetty frowned. "Jenny, you've got to learn not to be so busy. It's not healthy, running around like you do."

Without paying much attention to what Hetty had said, Jenny blurted out, "You'll never guess who I ran into at Dumbarton Oaks." She took the footstool, covered with a needlepointed robin's nest that Hetty had designed, and moved it over to the fireplace. She sat down to warm herself in front of the gentle flames.

"I give up. Who?" Hetty said, pouring herself a sherry.

"Steve Voight."

Hetty walked slowly toward Jenny so as not to spill her drink. The light from the fire played across the chain of her eyeglasses and cast a sunset glow on Hetty's pale skin, so smooth that it belied her eighty-four years. She was still a handsome woman. She combed her thick, silver-white hair into a bun as she had since her days as a ballerina. And her large, violet-gray eyes never ceased to sparkle. "Who's Steve Voight?" she asked.

"He's the one I told you about. He's lobbying for the farmers," she answered.

"The man who raises cattle?" Hetty asked, her interest rising.

"That's him." Jenny smiled, watching Hetty wrap her mohair shawl close over her shoulders as she settled into her armchair. The once vibrant maroon velvet upholstery was now dull and so worn it looked like leather. And the contour of Hetty's body was embedded into the chair, as were the teeth marks of the various cats Hetty had cared for during the years. Jenny knew it was hopeless to suggest buying a new chair. Besides, age had given the chair a character all its own, like Hetty herself.

"So, what happened at Dumbarton Oaks?" Hetty asked.

"He kissed me."

"Kissed you? Hmm."

"Look, I've got to get dressed for Anna's

party. Come upstairs with me. I need to talk to you."

Amber scurried after them and jumped up onto Jenny's bed. Her paws sank into the thick down quilt as she ran across the bed to where Hetty sat. Hetty looked around the room while gently stroking the cat curled up on her lap.

Jenny had been living in Hetty's upstairs apartment since she moved to Washington. She had fallen in love with it at first sight. Abundant light flowed over the treetops into the rooms, through tall and narrow dormer windows. And everywhere Jenny turned she saw the marks of craftsmen from an era long gone—the embossed brass doorknobs, the patterned parquet floors, the sunburst design around the ceiling light fixtures. Finding the apartment and Hetty had been a turning point for Jenny—her first stroke of luck after she had left Vance.

During the first couple of years when she and Anna were starting out, money was tight. She didn't have much to spend on home furnishings. But little by little, Jenny managed to create a French country look for her apartment. Though she could now afford a lot better, she changed nothing. She had grown as accustomed to her cheerful apartment as she had to her cocktails with Hetty. She didn't want either to change.

Their evening cocktail ritual had begun as

an occasional cup of tea when Jenny came home from work. Then one day Hetty asked if Jenny would prefer something stronger. When Jenny said that she would enjoy a glass of wine, it was then that she learned of Hetty's fondness for a glass of sherry at the end of the day. And their friendship blossomed despite an almost sixty-year difference in their ages.

"Would you believe he said I looked beautiful? I looked a mess!" Jenny said, pulling on a pair of black nylons.

"I'm glad he can see beyond your fancy clothes and made-up face," Hetty responded.

"He sure can. Things like that don't bother him in the least. Steve's the most down-to-earth man I've ever met."

"Imagine that! A down-to-earth man here in Washington. What a breath of fresh air!" Then she paused and said, "Jenny, something's bothering you."

Jenny sighed. "It's my job. I'm having doubts I never had before."

"What do you mean?"

"Well, up until now I've always felt good about what I do. I was really happy to see my clients improve their images. But it's different with Steve. I don't want him to change. And I'm beginning to wonder how important things like wearing the right clothes and using the right fork really are."

"Not very," Hetty said. "I've got a lot of

rich, blue-blooded friends who have superb manners and the personalities of dead fish."

"And that's what sometimes scares me, that I'm going to turn Steve into a dead fish. I know I can prime him so he can mingle with the upper echelon, join exclusive country clubs where they all tell the same jokes and wear the same bright golf pants."

Jenny dropped her hands between her knees and sat down next to Hetty. "I keep going back to what happened to me when I was with Vance," she went on. "While I was learning to do things properly, like not talking with my hands, my spirit was choking." She looked down at her hands, gracefully poised to express her next words. "Look, I still have trouble talking without my hands."

"So what? Do you know that in parts of Europe they are suspicious of people who don't talk with their hands?" Hetty reached over to Jenny's hands and stroked them as she often stroked Amber's paws. "Your hands are alive, like you. They reflect your warmth and tenderness—your readiness to reach out to others. So, relax and have more confidence in your natural appeal. Believe me, Steve is going to survive your image-making intact. And you know that."

Jenny smiled. "I do. He knows what he wants. Nothing is going to change that."

"Then why are you worried about Steve

turning himself over to you like your other clients do, to be trained as if they were little puppy dogs?" Hetty leaned forward in her chair to look more closely at Jenny. Then her look of concern vanished as a smile crept up her face. "You're not worried about falling in love with him, are you?"

"I loved once. And you know what happened to me."

"You think that was love?" Hetty shook her head. "Love grows—it doesn't smother."

"It smothered *me.* I'm not going to let that happen again."

"Do you really believe you can stop it?"

"Yes."

Hetty pressed down on the edge of the bed. "Sometimes, Jenny, I wonder about you. How long is it going to take you to understand what life is really like?"

"I thought I had a pretty good handle on it."

"Not when you talk like that. Do you think you can control something like love?"

"Yes—as far as I'm concerned, love is an act of will."

Hetty laughed out loud. "Rubbish!"

Jenny shrugged, not wanting to discuss it further. Already she found herself becoming anxious and nervous at the thought of being involved with a man again. She searched through her jewelry box until she found a medallion she had bought at a local craft show.

The face was a swirl of metals welded together. She liked it because the silvery blue tinged with bronze reminded her of the sky when the sun was setting over Dumbarton Oaks. That was all the jewelry she wore.

"You look smashing," Hetty said as Jenny got ready to leave. "Someday, Jenny, someone is going to take off that professional mask of yours and free your real self. Then you'll be absolutely irresistible—another Ingrid Bergman, or Katharine Hepburn, maybe—even a Gloria Swanson!"

Jenny feared that that someone might be very near. She remembered what Steve had said at Dumbarton Oaks about being glad he caught her with her mask off.

Chapter Two

"Nothing pleases that husband of mine," Mrs. Michel said. She had been in Washington a year. It was the first time she had ever lived outside of the Caribbean island where she was born. She was not adjusting well, so an acquaintance of her husband's had suggested Jenny's firm as a possible solution.

Mrs. Michel paced back and forth while Jenny listened with her elbows on her desk, her chin propped on her clasped hands. "I come to you as he wanted," Mrs. Michel ranted. "I do what you tell me to do, wear what you tell me to wear, so I will look like an ambassador's wife. I don't even recognize myself in the mirror anymore. I do all this. I leave my relatives and friends so he can be Mr. Big Shot." With her café-au-lait-colored skin, hazel eyes, and long straight black hair, Mrs. Michel could have passed for a *Vogue* cover girl. Except, at the moment, she had as much appeal as a pouting, whining, spoiled child.

Jenny was having difficulty concentrating on what Mrs. Michel was saying, because her mind kept wandering to Steve. The phone rang, interrupting Mrs. Michel's tirade. "Hello, Jenny? Chuck Jensen. That Steve Voight is dynamite. You've got to listen to this tape."

Jenny heard the cassette click and then Steve's voice: "We have enough acts of God to contend with without the government being another one. We know we can't do anything about tornadoes and droughts, but we *can* do something about an elected government that doesn't care about the farmer. It's about time Washington got its act together and represented the people—all the people, not just the fat-cat contributors."

"Fantastic," Chuck said, interrupting.

"Sure is. That's why you're my favorite speech writer. I wouldn't have trusted Steve in any other hands," Jenny said, delighted.

"Thanks, but I had nothing to do with it. That was him ad-libbing. It's incredible."

"Sure is," Jenny said, marveling at how strong and dynamic Steve sounded.

"Does this guy have any political ambitions?" Chuck asked.

"Not that I know of. He just wants to have enough clout to get things done."

"That he'll do. But I'd love to follow him on a campaign trail. He sure could make mincemeat out of those clowns up on the Hill if he ever wanted to. Keep working on him."

"Was that a special call?" Mrs. Michel asked as Jenny hung up the receiver.

"Huh? Oh, no. Just about a client."

"You looked so happy. I thought you got some good news."

Jenny could feel herself blush, and she tried to cover it up. "It *is* good news. He's doing quite well."

"You look very proud of him. Is he only a client?"

Jenny looked into Mrs. Michel's caring eyes and said, "I guess you could say a client friend." This time she could not control her blush.

"Nothing more?"

"It can't be anything more. Business and romance don't mix well."

"But how can you prevent it, if you care for each other? I'm sure he cares for you. How could he not? You are everything a man could want."

Jenny smiled. "You're too kind. But this is your time. We should be discussing your problems, not mine." She noticed how Mrs. Michel's face had softened, and how much prettier she looked.

Mrs. Michel shook her head. "You're the one who has been kind to me. I've thought of you as untouchable, and never dreamed I would be worthy of your confidence. I miss sharing problems with friends. No one here seems to do it. Everyone is so standoffish."

"Remember a few minutes ago when you were talking about not liking it here?" Jenny asked. Mrs. Michel nodded. "Well, if I were meeting you for the first time then, I'd probably be standoffish too. In fact, I'd be afraid of you, afraid you might bite my head off. If you look like that at parties, I can understand why you find yourself alone."

"You know, meeting people was not a problem for me on my island. I have known everyone there since I was a little girl. It was easy. But here, I don't even know how to begin," Mrs. Michel said.

"Begin with a smile. A smile is universal. Use yours, and you'll make as many good friends here as you have back home." Jenny saw Mrs. Michel's worried look. "But you're not ready to do that, are you?"

"What do you mean?" Mrs. Michel asked.

"You have to stop acting like a horse with blinders on. Get rid of your preconceived notion that you aren't going to be happy here. Because, consciously or unconsciously, you are fighting anything that might convince you otherwise. Instead of pining away for your homeland, you should be putting your energy into telling people about your country."

"That's my husband's job, not mine. I am only supposed to be a gracious hostess."

"I don't think there's any law against doing more. Not when an ambassador's wife has written an hilarious newspaper column on life in Washington as she sees it, and another from the Middle East has done more to elevate the public's image of Arab women and to popularize their cause than all the higher-ups put together."

"That's hard to imagine," Mrs. Michel said after Jenny had told her about several other wives who had been successful in their own right. "I guess I have some thinking to do."

"Remember," Jenny said, seeing a glimmer in Mrs. Michel's eye as she walked her to the door, "being sad can become a habit—but so can being happy."

Jenny returned to her desk, recalling the tape Chuck had played for her. Steve's voice was strong, the kind that marks a leader. She had been surprised to hear him speak with such force and conviction. He had always been gentle and soft-spoken with her. She wondered how many other sides there were to him that she didn't know.

The phone rang again. Jenny picked up the receiver. A voice said, "Remember me?" It was Steve.

"Of course—it's only been a day."

"A day too long."

"I bet you say that to all your lady friends," Jenny said, wondering how many he had.

"No, you're the first since…." His voice trailed off, and he changed the topic. "I was with Chuck Jensen this morning."

"I know, I was just talking to him."

"Oh?"

"He played a tape of you over the phone. He thinks you're dynamite."

Steve laughed as if that was ridiculous. "What did you think?"

"I agreed."

He was silent, then said, "How about that rain check? Is dinner on Saturday night okay?"

"Great!" The word escaped before Jenny could stop herself. *You fool!* she scolded herself. *Why did you say that? You should be making excuses not to go.* But now it was too late—she had said she'd go. And perhaps it was for the best. It would give her a chance to reestablish their business relationship.

"I heard there's an Italian restaurant in Georgetown that has really good food," Steve said.

"It sure does. It's one of my favorite places."

"You don't have to dress up, do you?"

"No, it's casual."

"Good."

Jenny got the feeling he preferred it that way, not so much because he wanted to be comfortable, but because he wanted to see her as she was at Dumbarton Oaks—out of office attire. Once again, with her mask off.

"Hetty, what in heaven's name is going on?" Jenny said when she got home from the office and saw Hetty seated behind her desk, dwarfed by piles of mail. Amber had been sleeping on top of some more letters scattered on the floor, and she awoke at the sound of Jenny's voice.

"They said I broke a record."

"Who's they?"

"The people at the magazine. They said my 'in search of ad got the most responses they ever had. Four hundred and twenty-six, to be exact."

"Hetty, at your age?"

"It's not for me, silly. I put it in for you."

"For me!"

"Thought you could use some male companionship."

"I'm getting some. You might like to know Steve is taking me out for dinner next Saturday night."

"Good, and you could use a little rehearsal. It's been so long since you've been on a date." Hetty grabbed a fistful of letters. "Here, take your pick."

"I really can't believe you're serious," Jenny said, annoyed by Hetty's grin.

"It's only practice. You're pretty rusty, you

know. I don't want you making a fool of yourself."

"Don't worry, I won't," Jenny said, holding back her resolution to make up some reason to give Steve why they shouldn't date again. She swiped a copy of the magazine off the table. "Do you know what those ads are like?" Jenny asked, quickly thumbing through the pages. "Hetty, this is absurd!" She plopped down into a swivel chair and moved her finger down the ad column. "Listen to these adjectives: 'witty,' 'charming,' 'passionate,' 'wily,' 'wacky,' 'fun-loving,' 'athletic,' and 'dynamic' I shudder to think what adjectives you dreamed up for me."

" 'Average.' "

"Average?" Jenny said, somewhat disappointed.

Hetty put on her eyeglasses. "Now, let me see," she said. "I've got a copy of that letter I wrote somewhere around here." She dug among the papers, as if feeling for a buried object. Jenny knew she did it to stretch out the suspense. "Oh, there it is, right under my nose." Hetty cleared her throat. " 'Average female in search of a nice, average man.' "

"That's it?"

"Yes, madam!" Hetty swept her arms over the piles of letters. "And here are your men. They're all clamoring for you."

"You know I'm not interested in this sort of thing," Jenny said, folding her arms. She shifted her weight. Hetty looked up over her bifocals at her. Outside, the sun had set while they had been talking. Only a small desk lamp with a rose silk shade lit the room. Jenny became aware of its light circling the two of them. She felt as if this circle was the boundary of her world; everything beyond was open darkness.

"Why not?" Hetty asked. "Where's your spirit of adventure?"

"You're impossible," Jenny said, getting up to fetch their drinks. Hetty's young mind never ceased to amaze her. Jenny's lips parted in a slight smile as she said to herself, *All you guys in those little envelopes—you don't want me. She's the one you'll have more fun with.* Jenny nervously poured Hetty's sherry, then some white wine for herself. In the background, she heard Hetty slitting open more envelopes.

"Cheers," Hetty said, taking her glass from Jenny. "None of these are marriage contracts, you know. They're just a way of introduction, just as good as meeting through a friend or on a plane."

"I've met someone. And I wish I hadn't. Already it's doing a good job of messing up my life. I had a hard time concentrating on my clients today."

"So forget your clients and have some fun." Jenny frowned at that. "Oh, Miss Prim and Proper," Hetty said, "how hard you've made your life!"

Chapter Three

"Anything new with the farming bill?" Jenny asked Steve when the waiter had finished taking their order.

"Not on the Hill. But there sure is a lot going on back home. I just can't understand why the legislators, even those who represent the farm belt, are shutting their eyes to how bad it is." He looked troubled. "It's even getting to my brother-in-law. He's having financial problems too. I've offered to help him out, but he won't let me."

"How come?"

"He said he doesn't want more money. He said that's when all his problems began, when the banks encouraged him to borrow so he could expand his livestock a few years back when everything was better. Now, with a couple of crop failures and last summer's drought, he's having trouble meeting payments. He said if he hadn't taken that one dumb loan, he'd be doing okay."

"Do you think he'll make it?"

"I don't know. Things look pretty grim. Sometimes bankruptcy is the only sane way out. But he doesn't want to file for it. It's hard. Hard on my sister, Kathy, too. She's worried about him. He used to be a pillar of strength, but lately he's been having trouble sleeping and flies off the handle at the littlest thing."

"That can be tough."

"You bet it can."

Someone called out Steve's name. Jenny turned around and saw a preppy-looking man in his late twenties walking toward them. "Hi, Jim," Steve said, standing up. "I'd like you to meet Jenny Foster."

"It's nice to meet you. Great guy you've got here," Jim said to Jenny. "He's honest as the day is long—salt-of-the-earth type. You know the kind I mean."

"Sure do," Jenny said. "I grew up with people like that."

"Where are you from?" Jim asked, glancing over his shoulder toward his friends, who were being seated at the other end of the restaurant.

"Oh, a small town in the Midwest, one no one ever heard of," Jenny said, noticing Steve's raised eyebrows.

"I'd better get going," Jim said, his friends waving him over. "Enjoy your dinner."

"It's hard to imagine that you come from a small town," Steve said, as soon as Jim was out of hearing range. "Are you a farm girl by any chance?"

"Yes, I am."

He shook his head. "Boy, I sure had you figured wrong. I thought you'd gone to finishing schools and all that stuff."

She laughed. "No, it was a far cry from that. But I must tell you that having grown up on a farm sure makes me appreciate what a farmer has to go through. And I think they're really lucky to have someone like you pushing for them." She sensed his pride in what she had said.

He started telling her a story about a neighbor who had to sell off some of his farmland to cover the medical expenses of his wife's cancer. With less land, he was making less, and he had to sell more land to pay the bills. "It's like being in quicksand," he said. "The more you struggle to get out, the deeper you sink."

Yes, she thought, his words having elicited her sympathy, *he's got the touch. With a little exposure, Steve Voight is going to be a well-known name in Washington.*

Jenny wondered about the man who had just stopped by. He seemed to think so highly of Steve. "Who is he?" Jenny asked.

"Jim Watson is an aide to Senator Maxwell. He's been a big help to me."

"It pays to know people like him."

"You bet. I've learned how important contacts are. Jim not only gets me appointments with the senator but also has his ear. I know very well that after I've given my spiel and left, the senator is going to tap Jim on his shoulder and ask him what I was talking about. I can count on Jim to understand the points I'm trying to make, and I'm glad he's one hundred percent behind me."

Steve reached across the table for her hand and gently squeezed her fingers. His eyes lingered on hers as he lifted his glass and nodded an unspoken toast to her. She smiled back. Never before had she felt so drawn to a man.

Steve winked at someone behind Jenny. "Someone else you know?" she asked without turning around.

"No, but she's flirting with me. A real doll." Jenny could just imagine the platinum-blond sexpot sitting behind her; Washington was filled with her type. Jenny turned around slowly, only to face an adorable one-year-old with a bib around her neck, her eyes glued to Steve.

The little girl leaned to the side of her highchair, offering Steve her soggy bread stick. A broad smile spread across her chubby face when she saw him bite into it. She cackled in delight when he gave her a fresh bread stick from their table. Watching Steve interacting with the little girl affected Jenny deeply. He certainly was special—very different from the men she had met in the past.

Still looking at the little girl, Steve said to Jenny, "I'd love to have children someday." Then he turned and looked at her. "Wouldn't you?"

"I suppose."

He appeared surprised that her answer was so vague. It surprised her too. But somehow she had never thought about having children. Growing up, she had loved being around them. But Vance had made it clear when he proposed to her that he didn't want any—he had said they would interfere with their social life. Jenny didn't understand why. They would have a maid, and the children would have nannies to care for them when she and Vance were away. But Jenny didn't question him because she had become too insecure around him to feel that what she wanted could count. She assumed Vance was right, as she had done in respect to almost everything else. She was so in awe of him. It wasn't until later that she understood why Vance didn't need a child. He already had one—her.

The waiter put down their plates in front of them. Yes, she *did* want children. But if she couldn't make the first step toward marriage, how could she ever make it to motherhood?

Jenny watched Steve eat. His table manners were excellent, showing good upbringing.

Good table manners were totally democratic—you didn't have to be rich or classy to have them. Jenny had found that how one ate was a good gauge of character. People who cared about others were quick not to give offense, and especially careful to keep their mouth closed when chewing and to avoid talking with their mouth full. They wanted those sharing their meal with them to enjoy their food too.

"Do you realize you're spoiling my appetite?" Steve asked, putting his fork down. He placed his hands flat on the red-and-white checked tablecloth, and leaned back in his chair, away from Jenny. She turned scarlet. "You've been watching everything I do," he said, irritated. "Didn't we finish our table manners session? I thought you said I passed with flying colors."

"You did."

"So why do I feel like you're putting me through it again?"

"Sorry," Jenny said, embarrassed for having violated her own good manners training. "It must be an unconscious carry-over from my job." This was the perfect moment to tell him that dating a client was not going to work, without going into any further details concerning her reasons for wanting to avoid all romantic relationships. She felt it was better to end this before it had a chance to begin.

But just as she was about to tell him, he said

with a smile, "I guess I have to remind you again that this is after hours?" And before she could stop him, he leaned over and kissed her. It was a light, gentle kiss. "Does that do the trick?" he asked, his eyes smiling at her.

Unfortunately it did, but she didn't dare tell him. She looked down at his plate, lost for words. "Would you like to try some?" Steve asked, pushing his plate over to her.

"It's delicious," she said, sampling his pasta. He refilled their glasses with Bardolino wine. They clicked their glasses together in a second toast, the claret luminous in the candlelight.

"You know," Jenny said, "for someone coming from the Midwest, you sure have an educated palate."

Steve laughed. "Mary can take credit for that. She was a real gourmet cook. It's too bad that so few of the folks back home were keen on trying different foods. It's funny—they'll think nothing of eating gizzards and Rocky Mountain oysters because they grew up with them. But they'll turn up their noses at something like stuffed breast of veal. They didn't care much for Mary's cooking." He had a faraway look as he spoke. "She saved her fancy cooking for when we were alone."

Jenny let him dwell on his thoughts. He seemed oblivious to her presence. This was the first time Steve had ever mentioned Mary to her. Obviously, she was someone very important in his life. Jenny let several minutes pass before she dared to ask, "Who's Mary?"

"My wife."

"Your wife!" Jenny said, gasping. Steve was still lost in thought and seemed unaware of her concern. He looked down at his hands and said, "She died seven years ago."

"What happened?" Jenny asked, hoping she wasn't prying too much.

Steve didn't seem to mind. "She was hit by a drunk driver."

"How awful."

"It was. I didn't think I would ever get over it."

"But you have," she said. Steve shrugged. He looked so sad. "I'm surprised you haven't remarried," she went on, hoping to lighten his spirits. "You'd be a great catch for someone."

He smiled slightly. "I don't know about that. But Mary was a special woman. Replacing her would be hard." He took a sip of his wine. In a less somber tone, he said, "Besides, there aren't many single women back home. There's Edith—she's the church organist. But Edith is so fat and hypercritical. She's the only one I know whose eyebrows are permanently frowning."

"I can see that Edith wouldn't do."

"The only one left is Tillie. But every time she dates a man, she ends up having a nervous breakdown."

Jenny paled. That was her—*she* was Tillie.

"Are you all right?" Steve asked.

"I think I need some air," Jenny said, feeling faint. Steve quickly called the waiter over and handed him more than enough money to cover the bill and tip.

Outside, Jenny took a deep breath of the cool, late-March air that hinted the earthy scents of the coming spring. She felt steadier. She didn't have to tell him about her engagement to Vance, or why she had broken it—not unless they were in love. And she felt safe in her determination not to let that happen. She looked at Steve.

"Feeling better?" he asked.

"Yes, I guess the wine got to me," she said, fibbing. "I'm not used to more than two glasses. The fresh air feels so good. Do you mind if we walk a little?"

"Mind? It'd be a pleasure to walk by your side."

She took the arm he offered her. Their rhythmic steps echoed as they strolled down brick sidewalks, dimly lit under old-fashioned street lamps, past attached row houses emitting cozy glows.

Jenny saw a couple inside one of the houses, sitting on a couch and watching TV with a bowl of popcorn between them, their feet up on a cocktail table. She let her guard down for a second and thought how nice it would be if she and Steve were the ones inside that house, instead of outside in the cool of the night. She noticed Steve looking at the couple too. She saw the sad look on his face, and she sensed he was thinking of Mary.

He turned toward her and took her in his arms, pressing her against his chest. He kissed her forehead lightly, taking her chin in his hand; then, sweeping back her hair, he kissed her lips. She couldn't stop her heart from beating at his touch. She could see the smile on his face as they drew apart.

"How about some dessert?" Steve asked.

"We did miss out on that. Sounds good," Jenny answered.

They shared a huge slice of Black Forest cake at a sidewalk café. And Steve offered to pour cream into Jenny's coffee—a charming touch on his part that made her feel very special. The way he did it, so naturally, as if he did it every day, told her so much about him and Mary.

She pictured the two of them in their farmhouse, with snow falling outside, sitting by the fire after having eaten a dinner they had cooked for themselves, and him pouring cream into Mary's coffee. Words would not have been necessary. In their love, just being together would have been enough. Her heart ached.

"What are you thinking?" Steve asked, taking a sip of his espresso.

"That you're a very special person."

"Coming from you, that's impressive," he said, smiling. Jenny smiled back. "I've really enjoyed tonight," he said, taking her hand. He drew her fingers to his lips and kissed the tips softly, reluctant to relinquish them. His eyes stayed on her hand as he lowered it back to the table. Still clasping her hand, he looked up into her eyes.

"I've enjoyed it too," Jenny said. Amid the quiet murmur of the café and the low light, she looked down at his fingers, long and tapered like a piano player's, gently stroking her wrist. She felt lightheaded from the wine, the good meal, and his nearness, his touch. Seeing the smile on his face, she struggled to reconfirm her resolution not to disturb her life by falling in love with Steve. But for the moment she would allow herself the enjoyment of his company. Hetty was right. It was nice being with a man, especially one with whom she felt relaxed. She felt none of the nervousness she had felt with Vance. But would her dreadful anxiety return if she and Steve were more serious? She didn't know. For the moment, however, she felt safe, and she cared about nothing else.

She watched carefully as he folded his napkin properly and placed it back on the table by his plate. "You're working again," he scolded gently.

"Just a little," she teased, slipping her arm into his as they rose to leave.

"Hmm," he said, helping her into her coat. "What's the perfume you're wearing?"

"Ombre Rose. It's my favorite."

"It's mine now too." He smiled and opened the door for her.

"You look chipper," Hetty said as Jenny brought in the Sunday newspapers from the front door. "I gather things went well last night."

"Mmm. Yes."

"Well, then I guess you won't be needing this," Hetty said, pulling a letter from the pocket of her satin quilt robe.

"What's that?"

Hetty waved the letter like a flag. "The best response to my personal-column ad. I finished reading them late last night, and this one is by far the winner." Hetty reached for her eyeglasses. "Want me to read it to you?"

"Go ahead," Jenny said, knowing Hetty would anyway.

Hetty smiled and cleared her throat. " 'Dear average lady,' " Hetty began, then looked up at Jenny. "Remember that's how I identified you in my ad, as an average lady?" Jenny nodded, and Hetty continued, " Tor want of a better name, I call you that. I could not bring myself to write Dear P. O. Box 173. I'm not one to read the personal columns, although I suspect others will say the same. But it's true, and I consider it luck that made my dear great-uncle bring your ad to my attention. I could not resist answering your letter, because I, like you, would like to meet someone nice. I suppose I should begin with my description. I'm very average—five-ten, brown hair, brown eyes, about one hundred sixty pounds. I've enclosed my picture.' " Hetty handed it to Jenny.

"He's gorgeous."

"Above average, I'd say."

"Look at his smile—so natural—no phony posing like a model. You should see some of the other photos. One was of a guy lifting weights and he was built like Woody Allen."

Hetty smiled and went back to reading the letter. " 'As for my interests, I've tried a lot of different sports, but again I'm average in all and really am not overly enthusiastic about any. I guess I enjoy swimming most, but only when I'm near a beach. I like walking a lot, but slowly. I like to read, but my taste leans toward popular fiction. I guess I do what most people do—go to the movies, eat out once in a while. I do like to try new things and really can't think of anything I don't like to do.

" 'As for my being nice, that's up to you to decide. I'd really like to meet you, and I'm leaving it to you to choose the time and place if you are interested in meeting me. If not, I hope you find someone nice, anyway.' And he signed it, 'George Mahoney.' So, Jenny, what do you think?"

"It's okay."

"It's more than okay. Why don't you give him a try?"

"It's just like ordering from a catalog."

"So what? Where's your spirit of adventure?"

"Out to lunch," Jenny said, sorting the Sunday papers.

"Well," Hetty said, holding up her letter, "if you won't answer this poor lovelorn guy, I suppose you won't mind if I do?"

Jenny put the newspaper aside and looked at her, not too taken aback. Hetty was game for almost anything. "Be my guest," she said.

"May I have a picture of you to send him?"

Jenny looked at her as if she were a naughty child. Hetty shrugged off Jenny's rejection and began composing her letter to George Mahoney while Jenny read the papers. "How do you think this sounds?"

"Nothing doing," Jenny said, raising the style section of the newspaper so Hetty couldn't see her face. "I'm staying out of this."

Chapter Four

Jenny entered the conference room of the Royal Hotel. The morning panel discussion hadn't started yet. She joined the business executives, lobbyists, and lawyers milling around the buffet table, and helped herself to a croissant and a glass of orange juice. Steve had asked her to come. He was one of the panel speakers, and he wanted her to evaluate his performance.

Across the room, she could see Steve shaking hands and patting backs like a seasoned politician. She couldn't help but be proud of him, though she had very little to do with the grace and charm he exuded—he was born with that. There was absolutely nothing she could recommend to improve his style.

Steve smiled at everyone who came his way. But when he spotted Jenny, his smile seemed to light up even more. She knew hers did, and she feared everyone in the room would notice.

But when she looked around, no one seemed to be paying any attention.

Steve immediately came over to her. "Did you just get here?" he asked.

"No, I've been here a little while."

"Then why didn't you come over to me?"

"I was watching you operate."

"Oh," Steve said, trying to look worried. "How did I do?" But his budding smile showed that he knew he was handling himself well.

"Wonderfully! Just like I expected," Jenny said. His smile broke out. "Really, Steve, it's a waste for me to be here."

"No, it isn't. I need to hear you say things like that. It builds up my self-confidence."

She knew he was playing with her. "There's nothing wrong with your self-confidence."

"Wait, you'll see." Someone called out to get Steve's attention. It was Jim Watson, the man whom she had met at the Italian restaurant.

"Did you get a chance to see Senator Maxwell?" Jim asked Steve.

"Not yet."

"He wants to talk to you. He's over there."

"Come on," Steve said, reaching for Jenny's hand. He smiled when she pulled it away. Jenny knew it didn't matter to Steve, but holding hands was not very professional.

Steve introduced Jenny to Senator Maxwell. "Foster and Pitta," the senator mumbled to himself, seeming to have difficulty placing the name of her firm. "Isn't that an image-consulting outfit?"

"Yes," Steve answered before Jenny could.

"Got any clients on the Hill?" the senator asked Jenny unabashedly.

"It's not our policy to divulge who our clients are," Jenny answered, finding his cigar smoke sickening.

"So I guess I can't ask you if Steve is one of your clients?" Senator Maxwell quizzed Jenny.

"I sure am." Again, Steve answered quickly, much to Jenny's displeasure.

"Really?" the senator asked, showing positive interest.

"We're only in the preliminary stages of trying to evaluate areas in need of improvement," she said. "But as far as I can tell, Steve really doesn't need my help."

Steve smiled broadly. "See what she can do in just a couple of lessons, Senator? You should have seen me when I first came into her office wearing cowboy boots!"

"It's hard to imagine you in cowboy boots." The senator rubbed his chin. "Hmm, Miss Foster, maybe I could have one of your cards." Jenny gave it to him reluctantly. "I hear that a lot of people are turning to folks like you for advice."

A stranger interrupted them, wanting to talk privately to Senator Maxwell for a minute. The senator excused himself, saying to Jenny and Steve, "You know how it is. Everyone has something he wants to tell his senator." Jenny smiled politely, fully appreciating that the senator loved every bit of the attention he got.

She was glad to be rid of this man who in many ways reminded her of Vance, although Vance was a lot smoother. They were both used to being catered to and getting their way; but while the senator had advanced into his position of power, Vance had been born into it. Everyone, from his friends to his chauffeur, snapped to attention for Vance. He had expected Jenny to do so too. He never seemed to recognize how unnatural such behavior was.

But no one had acted otherwise with him. From infancy, his every need and desire had been immediately met. Making concessions was foreign to him—he had no idea that someone might not want what he wanted. And at twenty-one, Jenny hadn't yet gained the self-esteem and confidence to express her own opinions and feelings. She tried going where he wanted to go, wearing what he chose, even eating and drinking what he selected. Maybe another woman could live that way, but in the end she couldn't.

No one could understand how Jenny could give up such a fantastic, caring man. People in Vance's circle concluded that she wasn't the marrying kind. Her father was embarrassed and furious when she broke down the night before her wedding and said she couldn't go through with it. He idolized Vance and thought she was crazy to give up the security she'd have with him. Her father had stormed out of her room, shouting back at her, "Don't you ever dare think of marrying again!" Jenny had been too shattered at the time to verbalize her reasons. Her mother had said nothing. Ever since then, a distance lay between Jenny and her family.

Steve bent over and whispered in Jenny's ear, "See how nice this trip is working out for you? Now you have a potential client."

Jenny leaned away from him, wondering what people might think, and said softly under her breath, "I didn't come here looking for clients."

An announcement was made that the discussion was about to begin. Jenny sat in the back of the audience, listening to Steve and another farmers' representative, several industrialists, Senator Maxwell, and a congressman banter back and forth. Steve was carrying himself well without shouting, and was delivering his thoughts with perfect timing, sometimes pausing or emphasizing certain words to maximize their effect.

"Times are changing," an industrialist said, directing his statement at Steve. "Maybe it's time the farmers look for something else to do."

"It's not just a matter of changing jobs. It's more than that—it's their *lives.*" There was fire in Steve's eyes. "Do you know how much work it took to till our soil and get something to grow out of it? I'm not talking about the rich peat you find here in the East. I'm talking about soil so barren that it's almost white. You can scrape it off the ground like peeling paint.

"Generations and generations of sweat and tears have gone into making it produce. It's important that you know that," he said, rapping his fist on the desk in front of him, "because when a farmer fails, he fails not only himself and his family, but his father and grandfather and all those before him. They were the people who fought off the Indians, held out through the dust storms, and struggled during the Depression to pass their land on to him for safekeeping. It's his family he's failed—all of them. That's a heavy load to bear."

Steve was a man of deep feelings. Jenny found her heart beating fast, caught up in the emotion in his voice. The rustle she heard in the audience told her it wasn't her biased opinion that was making her feel that way. Others, too, were reacting favorably to Steve. She had no doubt that he could be a real mover and shaker in Washington.

* * *

"Howdy, stranger," Jenny said later that afternoon when Anna entered her office.

"I'm beat," Anna said, sinking into a swivel chair. She kicked off her pumps and massaged her feet. "These trips back and forth to the Middle East are beginning to get to me." She took a look at her watch. "Do you know it's been twenty-four hours since I've been to bed?"

"Then why didn't you go straight home from the airport?"

"I'm headed home—I just thought I'd check in first and see if anything important is going on."

"Nothing that can't wait till you get some sleep," Jenny said, watching her yawn.

Anna had managed to outwit their competitors and walk off with a contract to put together commercials on the Middle East, to be televised during the Summer Olympics. This was a big step for their firm—a branching out into overseas markets. Jenny's head spun with thoughts of all the future opportunities this could bring. This was a marked change from her first reaction, when she was reluctant and concerned that they might be taking on too much. But Anna wanted to give it a try. And Jenny felt it was only right to give Anna her full support.

"Will you be wrapping it up soon?" Jenny asked.

"I hope so," Anna answered, stretching. "Being a woman in that country is hard. Women are so restricted. You have to be careful to dress modestly."

"You shouldn't have to worry about that. I've never seen you wear anything the least bit immodest," Jenny said, noting that no one could possibly object to the tasteful Calvin Klein suit Anna was wearing.

Anna laughed. "Not by their standards. Sometimes I think it would be easier if I covered myself with a black veil."

"I can't believe you'd ever do that."

"You want to bet? Jenny, in the Middle East, even a belt is considered indecent!"

"A belt?"

"Yes, a belt."

"For heaven's sake, why?"

"It shows off a woman's waist." Anna shook her head. "Believe me, I would welcome the invisibility a black veil offers, anytime. If only I knew where I could buy one."

"Are there other problems?" Jenny asked, concerned. Anna had never mentioned anything like this before.

"Nothing major. Just an occasional hiss like I'm Satan's serpent. And many looks of disdain." Anna sighed. "All I can say is I sure was glad when the Concorde landed and I heard the pilot say 'Welcome home.'"

"I'm glad you're home too. But if it's getting to you, we can drop the whole thing."

"Not on your life. I've worked too hard to let little things like this stop me from seeing this project through to completion." Jenny smiled, admiring Anna's spunk. Anna had every right to feel proud of what she had accomplished.

"By the way," Anna asked, "how are things coming along with Steve Voight?"

"So far, I'm safe," Jenny answered, knowing Anna was referring to her off-hours relationship with him.

"What is that supposed to mean?"

"You know I don't want to get involved again, not after what happened with Vance and me.

"Not all men are like Vance," Anna said, yawning. "I've always said it's your guilt over breaking off your engagement that's made you run from other men. You don't feel you're worthy of a second chance."

It wasn't guilt, but an inherent psychological weakness on her part that was the problem, Jenny thought. "I don't want a second chance. I'm happy being single. Just the idea of marriage can give me the willies."

"You had the willies only once. You've never let yourself get close enough to anyone to see if you would have them again."

"Willies is a mild word. It was a major

breakdown. I dropped twenty pounds in no time at all."

Acquaintances had blamed Jenny's nervousness on excitement over the wedding. But it got worse. She could barely eat; soup was all she could keep down. The seamstress would yell at her to gain some weight, because her wedding gown would be ruined if it had to be taken in once more. Jenny would break down in tears.

The morning before the wedding she was a nervous wreck, trembling in her bed. Vance's family doctor prescribed tranquilizers. It was then that she realized she would have to spend her whole life tranquilized if she was to live with Vance. By that night, she drew up what little courage she had left and called off the wedding. "I'm not going to risk that again," Jenny said to Anna.

Anna tried to stifle another yawn. "Are you sure of that?"

"Yes. After all, I really don't know of anyone, outside of you and Joe, who have fallen in love and stayed in love. Not even my parents. I never saw them touch or kiss each other. They showed each other respect, but I saw nothing more in their eyes. Their eyes never reflected pleasure and joy in each other, just acknowledgement of the other's presence."

"Nothing's perfect, Jenny. Love is a very

frail thing. Didn't someone once say: 'Be more careful of love than of anything'?"

"That's right. It can be like a wasp's sting, sometimes even fatal."

"I don't think that's the analogy the person intended. But maybe your way is better; staying in love isn't always easy." Anna gave a wide yawn.

"That's it," Jenny said, pulling her out of the chair. "You're going home to bed. And take tomorrow off."

"Maybe I will. I've been gone so much I think Joe's beginning to forget he has a wife."

No sooner had Anna shuffled out the door then the phone rang. It was Steve, and he sounded upset. "Jenny, I'm heading back home."

"Is something wrong?"

"Yes." There was a pause, as if he was trying to compose himself. Then he said very softly, "My brother-in-law killed himself."

Jenny was so stunned that for a second she couldn't talk. Her heart grieved for him. "I'm so sorry," she managed to say.

"Oh, Jenny! It just doesn't make sense. If only these farmers weren't so attached to their land."

"Was he going to lose it?"

"Yes, he had filed his bankruptcy papers yesterday. Kathy found him hanging in the hayloft this morning."

"How awful for her!"

"She was so distraught she could hardly talk when she called me. She had to put a neighbor on the phone to tell me what happened. I'm flying out there this afternoon."

"Is there anything I can do?"

"Yes, get me into shape as fast as you can, so I can get that farming bill through before another farmer kills himself."

"Don't worry about that right now."

"I can't help but worry. Look, I've got to hurry and pack."

"How long do you think you'll be gone?"

"Until I think I can leave Kathy alone. I'll call you from there."

"Take care." Jenny hung up, wishing she could go with him. Despite what she had just said to Anna, she found herself wanting to be by his side, comforting him.

She attempted to go through the file of Sally Mitchell, her next client, but she had trouble concentrating. Already she felt as if her spirit were departing with Steve. She found herself imagining him getting into a cab, arriving at National Airport, and boarding the plane. She was picturing him meeting his sister when Gladys, her secretary, buzzed her to say Sally Mitchell had arrived. Jenny took a few minutes to draw forth her professional composure before she went out to greet Sally.

The first time she had met Sally, Jenny

couldn't believe that the petite woman standing before her was the same Sally Mitchell whose weekly syndicated newspaper column had earned her the reputation of a lady with an acid pen. Conservatively dressed, with her wavy gray hair cut short, she looked more like an upper-middle-class suburban housewife to Jenny—someone who would choose flower arranging as a creative outlet rather than slashing her creative sword through political jargon and biases to reveal the truth, as this pleasant and soft-spoken lady had done.

Recently, a major TV network had hired Sally Mitchell as an interviewer for its morning news show, and she was failing miserably at it. Sally was the reverse of Jenny's usual case—she already had a public image, so there was no need to build one for her. The problem was to help Sally match it. Jenny had arranged speech lessons for her to make her voice more forceful, and had worked on trying to give her a more imposing demeanor, all without much success. And Jenny was at a loss as to why things just weren't clicking.

This afternoon, Jenny had scheduled a taping of a mock interview during which Sally would question her. Jenny hoped that later, when reviewing the tape, she might be able to observe something—a mannerism or some other subtlety she hadn't seen before.

But as soon as Jenny shook Sally's hand, she

could tell something was bothering her. "I'm backing out," Sally said.

"Why? You haven't given yourself much of a chance."

"I know. But this whole thing's a mistake. I should have listened to my gut reaction. Instead, I let them convince me it would be a good change for me. I thought it might be too, with David gone and everything." Sally detected Jenny's confusion as to who David was, and explained he was her husband. "He died two years ago," Sally said, "and I'm still trying to get over it."

Sally's words brought to the surface the sorrow Jenny felt for Steve and his sister, and Jenny had to fight back her welling tears. She couldn't cope with the pain Sally and Kathy shared. She just wasn't emotionally strong enough to handle it, or perhaps even to handle being a wife. Being alone had proved best for her.

Sally's voice broke into Jenny's thoughts. "I thought that getting out from behind my typewriter and into the spotlight and the activity would be good for me. But it wasn't."

"Maybe you haven't given it enough time," Jenny said, resolving again to detach herself from Steve. It was the wise thing to do.

"More time would be the worst thing. Fortunately, I've realized that before it was too late."

"But…."

Sally raised her hand to stop Jenny from talking. "I know you're quite capable of turning me into the crackerjack, fast-talking and -thinking interviewer the station wants. But if I let that happen, I'm afraid I'm going to lose my writing skills."

"Oh, I doubt that."

"I don't. My writing is a slow, muddled process. It doesn't come rapidly, but in escaping bubbles of feelings and insights. As aggressive as the finished story might appear, the beginning is quite meek—a fragment of a thought. I have to observe people closely, read their faces for the twitches and blinks that speak to my subconscious. Above all, I have to hear what they say.

"I have worked hard at perfecting these skills. Now they've become my problem, because I automatically lapse back into these habits while I'm interviewing a guest on TV. I lose myself, listening and putting myself in the other person's place. I know I shouldn't do that, because when they're finished with my question, I need an extra second to get my bearings and come up with my next question."

She sighed. "I know that while they're talking, I should be thinking up a clever comeback to throw them off guard, to get them to blurt out the truth before they've thought of a lie. But I can't do that and listen at the same time.

And if I can't listen, I can't write." Sally's whitened knuckles reflected the determination Jenny heard in her voice. "My writing is as vital to me as my speech. I don't want anything to mess it up."

"I don't want that either," Jenny said. "I've missed reading your column too much to think that you'd never return to it."

Sally smiled. "I'll be telling the people at the station that I want out. I've been away from my typewriter too long, and it's getting on my nerves."

Jenny was glad when they shook hands and agreed to meet soon for lunch. She had gotten to like Sally as a person, respecting her intelligence and honesty, and she was happy to lose her as a client if it meant gaining her as a friend.

Chapter Five

Steve had been gone almost a month, and Jenny's resolution to detach herself from him was increasingly difficult for her to keep. He had called the minute he arrived on the farm. He said he was concerned about his sister, having known what she was going through. And Jenny was concerned about Steve; he sounded so tired and sad. She couldn't let him down, not at a time like this—she had to be there to listen to him. He called every day thereafter, and Jenny's heart leaped every time she picked up the phone and heard his voice. Her mind told her she shouldn't be accepting all his calls, but she couldn't help it.

From their phone conversations, Jenny learned that both of Steve's parents were dead. He was the only one Kathy had, now that Chip was dead. Kathy was coming along—at least he had gotten her to eat again. He talked a lot about the farmers' bill. Jenny guessed that concentrating on getting the bill passed was Steve's way of diffusing his anger over his brother-in-law's needless death.

The intercom buzzed.

"Yes, Gladys," Jenny said.

"Jack Ross's secretary just called. She said he won't be able to make his two-o'clock appointment with you. Some big deal has come up with a Swiss bank, and he had a plane to catch at noon. He sends his regrets."

"That's fine. I can use the afternoon to get caught up on some paperwork after I have lunch with Harrison and McLeod."

"Are those lawyers treating you well?"

"Very well. They're treading in new territory with us. But after seeing how image makers can help, they're more appreciative of what we can do."

An invigorating warmth heated the early-April air as Jenny and the lawyers said good-bye outside the restaurant. To Jenny's surprise, the lawyers were eager to sign on, and her lunch had turned out to be a leisurely one.

Waiting for a cab, she shed her gray wool jacket. She thought of all the work she had on her desk and of the cherry blossoms in full bloom around the Tidal Basin she had passed on her way to the restaurant. An empty cab approached, but she didn't raise her arm to hail it.

She called Gladys from a public phone. "Anything special going on?" she asked.

"Steve called."

"What did he have to say?"

"Just that he was heading back."

"When?"

"He didn't say. He said he'd call you later tonight."

Jenny wondered if he'd be in Washington by evening. She hoped so. She wanted to see him again, to know he was all right. "Anything else?"

"No, things are real quiet. Guess everyone must be out with spring fever."

Jenny laughed. "I've got it too. Look, Harrison and McLeod are officially our clients as of today, and I think I deserve the rest of the day off for that."

"You sure do. That's quite a coup. Anna will be glad."

The Tidal Basin was a maze of people swarming among the Japanese cherry trees and along the sidewalk that encompassed the blue water of the basin, sparkling in the sunlight. Jenny could hear birds singing and cameras clicking. Couples, hand in hand, strolled among flakes of delicate pink petals, almost white, falling in the breeze. Jenny was one of the few walking alone, and she wished Steve was with her to enjoy this land of enchantment.

A little way ahead, Jenny saw an elderly

couple sitting side by side on a park bench, looking out over the water. The gentleman looked very dapper in a navy blazer with a burgundy ascot. She couldn't help noticing his handsome mustache and wavy silver hair. His hands were crossed on top of a walking cane that rested between his feet. He was leaning toward the woman he was listening to, so Jenny couldn't see her too well until she came near.

"Hetty!" she cried in amazement.

"Jenny!" Hetty said, every bit as surprised as Jenny, although she recovered more quickly and added, "I'd like you to meet George Mahoney."

"George Mahoney?" Jenny said, half to herself. His name sounded familiar.

"He's the one who wrote the best response to my 'in search of ad." Hetty looked at her. "Remember?"

"But the picture…."

"Oh, that was my nephew," George answered. "I showed him the picture Hetty sent of you. But at the time, I didn't know Hetty was the one who had written to me. I thought it was you, and that the picture was of Hetty. I mean whoever wrote back to me. My, it does get confusing!"

Jenny squinted at Hetty, annoyed that she had taken the liberty of sending her picture. Hetty kept her eyes down to avoid looking at

Jenny. But Jenny could tell she was trying not to laugh.

"What a pity that my nephew wouldn't even consider looking at your picture. You're so lovely," George said with such a charming smile that Jenny could understand why he had apparently captivated Hetty. "But, alas, he would have nothing to do with my little match-making. I just don't know where his sense of adventure is."

Jenny smiled, recalling that Hetty had said something similar to her. *You're two kindred souls,* she said to herself. And in her pleasure of seeing them together, she forgave Hetty for mailing her picture.

"I'm sure glad he left me to answer the letter," George said, taking Hetty's hand and kissing it lightly. "Because now I've gotten to meet Hetty, who is 'as fresh as is the month of May.' "

Hetty blushed like a young girl as he described her in Chaucer's words. Jenny couldn't remember ever seeing her blush before. "When George returned your picture," Hetty explained to Jenny, "apologizing so much to me, thinking that I was you, I felt bound to write back and tell him that we were both guilty of the same deception. Well, one thing led to another—and here we are."

"You mean this is your first date?" They

both nodded. "And I'm walking in on you. How awful of me!"

"Why, not at all," George said gallantly. "I'm thrilled to meet you. After all, you are the one who brought Hetty and me together."

"Well, I'm glad I did. And I'll leave you now to enjoy the blossoms," Jenny said, winking, "and each other."

Jenny walked several blocks away from the Tidal Basin before she spotted a cab. "Taxi!" she and another man called out at the same time. She turned, astonished to see Steve coming around the corner with a carry-on bag slung over his shoulder.

"Jenny!" He waved, running to her. He dropped his bag and embraced her. He was finally with her again—and she realized how much she had missed him.

"Where to, folks?" the taxi driver shouted impatiently while horns honked at him for blocking traffic.

"Where are you headed?" Steve asked Jenny.

"Just home."

"Want to go to my place so I can drop off my bag? It will give us a chance to talk." Jenny nodded, and Steve gave the cab driver directions. Steve looked thinner and had dark circles under his eyes. But his face shone when he looked at her, and she couldn't help but be glad to see his smile again.

"You got off early today," he said, putting his arm around her.

"I caught spring fever and decided to take the afternoon off. I went over to see the cherry blossoms."

"I was just there too. I was on my way back from the airport and saw them from across the river. The taxi driver told me they last at most three or four days. So I had him drop me off so I could take a look.

"I didn't know until this morning that I'd be back. Something's come up on the Hill. I tried to call you, but you were out of the office."

"I know. Gladys relayed your message. I'm glad you're back."

He took her hand and said, "You know, when I was walking around the Tidal Basin just a little while ago, all I could think of was how much nicer it would have been if you were with me."

Jenny wanted to say that she was thinking the same thing, but she was afraid to, and she barely smiled at him as she turned and looked out the window to avoid his gaze.

The taxi came to a stop. Steve offered his arm for Jenny to lean on as she stepped out of the cab. She found herself standing in front of a boat yard. "Where do you live?" she asked him.

"Over there," he said, pointing to rows of

yachts, in various sizes, docked on the Potomac River behind a chain-link fence.

Steve rang a buzzer by the locked gate. A tall, burly security guard came out from a trailer office on the river side. He smiled at Steve and unlocked the gate, saying, "Glad to see you're back, Mr. Voight."

Jenny followed Steve down a pier leading toward a cluster of houseboats. Steve's was the last one at the end. "It's so quiet here," she said, hearing only the waves swishing against the moss-covered bulkhead.

"That's why I like it. It's like being on the farm. I expect it won't be so quiet, though, in the summer. I don't know how I'm going to like it then." He braced the side of his houseboat against the dock to make it easier for her to step onto its deck. Then he opened the sliding glass doors and showed her into the living room. He let his bag fall to the floor, and he stared at her.

"Why are you looking at me like that?" she asked.

"Like what?"

"Like you're seeing a beatific vision."

"I am." He took her into his arms and said, "Oh, Jen." He had never called her that before—no one had. The way he said it, softly, with a slight reverberation in the "n" like the faint ring of a distant chime, pleased Jenny's ear. "You have no idea how good it feels to be with you, how much I've missed you." She felt the smoothness of his face brushing her cheek, and smelled his familiar cologne. Leaning against his freshly starched shirt, she could feel how thin he had become. Then she heard his stomach grumble.

"I think it's trying to tell you something," Jenny said.

"I know, I'm starved. This is the first time I've been hungry in weeks. You're good medicine." Steve opened the refrigerator and shook his head. "Nothing much in here." Then he checked the freezer. "I've got a couple of pizzas. Is that okay with you?"

"That's fine." She looked around his full-sized kitchen. "This is quite a place."

"I'm glad you like it."

She stepped into the living room, which was separated from the kitchen by an L-shaped breakfast bar. "Who did the decorating? It looks like it's right out of *Better Homes and Gardens.*"

"The rich guy I rent it from. His wife thinks he's a fool for buying the boat, and she wants nothing to do with it. He never uses it. I think the only reason he's keeping it is to make her angry." He glanced at the wall clock. "Kathy should be home by now. I'd better give her a call and let her know I arrived in one piece." As he picked up the telephone receiver, he said, "Go ahead and make yourself comfortable.

There's a bathroom downstairs in case you'd like to freshen up."

Jenny wandered around while Steve talked to Kathy. At the opposite end of the living room was an alcove housing the steering devices and mechanisms of the houseboat—their highly polished wood and brass gleamed. From there she could see a deck lined with white vinyl-padded benches. She stepped outside to enjoy the warmth of the late-afternoon sun and breathe in the salty air.

She could smell the pizzas baking when she came back inside, and she found herself getting hungry too. Steve was still on the phone, telling Kathy that he had spoken with the bank and they shouldn't be bothering her for a while. "Don't worry about the money I left," he told her. "It will tide you over till things get settled."

Jenny didn't want to invade his privacy, though he didn't seem to mind, and decided to look for the downstairs bathroom he had mentioned. She found it adjoining a paneled bedroom. From the condition of the rooms, it looked as if Steve had left in a hurry.

When she came back upstairs, Steve was trying to lift the pizza tray from the oven with the telephone receiver braced between his ear and shoulder.

"Here, let me do that for you," she whispered.

Steve held the phone cord back for Jenny to get by while he talked to Kathy. "Another casserole! You better freeze that one. The last time I looked, the refrigerator was stacked with things people had brought over.... She's fine; she's here with me." Jenny turned around, realizing that he was referring to her. He must have told Kathy about her.

He winked at her and continued on the phone, "You'll meet her when you come here.... I know, but it will be good for you to get away. Besides, you promised me, and I've already planned some exciting things for us to do.... Never mind what they are—I want to surprise you. I'll call you tomorrow. Sleep well, and try to stay away from the sleeping pills if you can. It's better for you."

Jenny was touched by the kindness and tenderness he showed his sister. "How's Kathy doing?" she asked when Steve had hung up the phone.

"She's coming along. It's been rough for her."

"And for you too," Jenny said, noticing how much more his shoulders drooped. He looked over at her and nodded in agreement.

"I heard you mention to your sister about a visit to Washington."

"Yes, I hope in a couple of months. She doesn't think so, but she needs to get away from the farm for a while. I want you to meet her. I think you two would hit it off just fine." He kissed her lightly on her cheek. "Give me a minute to get into something more comfortable."

She set the table, managing to find what she needed, and was just lighting a lemon-colored candle when he came back upstairs. "That looks nice," he said, admiring her table setting. He was wearing a plaid shirt and dungarees. She smiled, thinking how nice *he* looked.

They sat down across from each other. "I wish I had more than pizza to offer you," he said, then bit into his slice.

"Why? It's absolutely delicious."

He shrugged. "I'm so hungry, I'm afraid I'm not a good judge. Right now, anything would taste good to me." He helped her to a second slice before taking another one for himself. Then he kissed her hand. The look in his eyes went straight to her heart. "Anything special happen while I was gone?"

She shared with him what she had done, her usual routine, and a few interesting tidbits. The setting sun was lowering under the violet dusk while he encouraged her to talk on, as if he wanted to recapture the time he had lost with her. The yellow candle grew more vibrant. "It's getting dark," he said, switching on the red metal light over the table as he cleared off their empty plates.

She smiled, watching him roll up his sleeves,

ready to do the few dishes. She dried the plates for him. "I think I'd better be going," Jenny said when they were done. "You look as if you could use some rest."

"I could. But please don't go right now." He seemed to really want her to stay. "I'll make us coffee."

She hesitated, then changed her mind and accepted his offer—but only for one cup.

He gingerly carried two filled coffee mugs over to the sofa where she was sitting, then turned on the stereo. He put his arm around her, and she snuggled against his chest, listening to the music and the beat of his heart. "I'd forgotten how good it feels to have a woman's head on my shoulder," he said, playing with her hair.

"I'm glad I'm that woman," Jenny said, wondering at the same time why she was saying that and why she had stayed. Where was her resolution to detach from him?

"Me too." A tune on the stereo caught his attention, and he started to hum. Then he lifted her hand, raising her from the sofa, and began to dance with her. He held her close, his arms clasped around her as they swayed together in rhythm to the melody. His cheek against hers felt as warm as the words he sang to her in a low voice, "'You are beautiful…you're everything….'"

The song ended, and he sang on until the

next song started. They danced to that, and the one after. Then he stopped and gently turned her face so he could look at her. "I love you, Jen," he said softly, bending toward her lips. Jenny pushed him away. "What's wrong?" he asked, puzzled. "Don't you love me too?"

She couldn't bear to look at him. "Steve, don't ask that of me."

"Why?"

"I can't."

"Can't love me?"

"Not you—not anyone," she said, biting her lip. "You don't understand."

"Try me."

Her shoulders dropped in frustration. "I loved once, and I swore I would never love again." She tried to sound determined. She looked into his eyes and read only tenderness and love.

"Maybe I'm rushing things too much," he said thoughtfully, and kissed her forehead. "I can wait until you change your mind."

"Steve." He looked at her. She met his eyes and said, "Don't count on that."

Chapter Six

Jenny sat across from Jack Ross, a real estate developer. He looked like Friar Tuck in a business suit and horn-rimmed glasses, devouring his lunch at an elegant private club in Georgetown. "How did your trip to Switzerland go?" she asked. Jack was hunched over, concentrating on his soup in its Wedgewood bone-china bowl. He bobbed his head up and down, signaling that it went well. *I won't be surprised if he lifts that bowl and drinks out of it,* Jenny said to herself. *What a way to be spending my birthday!*

"Sorry I had to cancel out on you. But," he said, taking a swallow of wine from a Baccarat bubble glass, "that bank deal was an important one."

"Things like that happen." Jenny said. She was glad he had canceled out, because that had given her the free afternoon when she saw the cherry blossoms and ran into Steve. She looked away from Jack for a moment, toward the lead glass French doors by their table. From where Jenny sat, she could see a copper statue of the god Pan, gleaming in the garden sunshine.

She found herself looking forward to seeing Steve tonight—they hadn't been together for weeks. He had thrown himself wholeheartedly into lobbying to get the bill through the House. Jenny knew he was doing it for Chip. But it didn't leave him with much time to see her. She knew she should be using his absence to forget about him, but it wasn't working. He called fairly often to see how she was. Those calls were short, made on the run between congressional meetings, but she looked forward to them, though she knew she shouldn't.

Before leaving to meet Jack Ross, Jenny had had a chance to glance at the morning paper, where she saw a picture of Steve on the front page. She'd skimmed the story that accompanied his photo. It was a synopsis of the pros and cons of the newly proposed legislation affecting agriculture. Steve's name appeared at least a dozen times in the two-page story. She'd put down the paper and leaned back, thinking about what she had read. The farmer had a powerful ally in Steve. She could appreciate even more why he was so busy; he seemed to be everywhere. And this powerful ally was taking her out tonight for her birthday.

Refreshed by the lovely sight of Pan trumpeting over a pool of water, as if to call the circling cluster of red tulips to open wider in praise of the midday sun, Jenny looked back at Jack Ross. What she saw made her sigh with frustration. "You should eat with your mouth closed," she said in as gentle a tone as she could.

"I can't."

"What do you mean, you can't?"

"I can't breathe with my mouth closed," he said. "I have a sinus condition."

Jenny shrugged. What on earth was she to do with this man? "I'm afraid you're going to have to practice doing it. That's one of the reasons your partners hired me. You need some polishing, and they think you're too good to let go."

"You know what the definition of a stuffed shirt is?"

"No," she said, annoyed that he didn't seem to be listening to a word she had said.

"My partners!" He laughed, then proceeded to cut his steak into bite-sized pieces. He looked up at her, and must have sensed her irritation. "You're very nice. I don't want to be a bother," he said. "If it makes you feel like you're earning your money, I'll try keeping my mouth closed, but only with clients."

"It's not going to work if you do it only with clients. You've got to practice. It's just like learning to play golf." She saw him wince. "You *did* sign up for lessons, didn't you?"

"Not yet," he said, avoiding her eyes like a naughty but unremorseful child.

"Why not?" Jenny was trying to control the rise in her voice. "I thought we discussed how important golf is in getting business contacts."

"It's only important here," he said. "Besides, it cuts too much into my free time." He finished his steak, then looked at her plate and asked, "Are you going to finish your shrimp salad?"

She shook her head.

"Well, it's too good to waste." He slid her leftovers onto his plate.

At least she'd be having a pleasant dinner with Steve tonight. He had set the date with her a week ago, but he wouldn't tell her where they were going. He wanted to surprise her. At the time, she hadn't connected it with her birthday since she knew she hadn't told him when that was. But this morning a special-delivery package had arrived at her office. Inside was the largest bottle of Ombre Rose perfume she had ever seen, a birthday gift from Steve. She had tried calling him immediately to thank him, but he was out of his office for the day. No matter, they'd be together tonight, and she'd find out how he knew that it was her birthday and that Ombre Rose was her favorite perfume.

"What's the matter?" Jack asked, catching Jenny off guard.

"Nothing."

"You were smiling like you were thinking of your boyfriend." She felt herself blush. "Getting married?"

"No."

"Why not?"

"I don't think that really should concern you."

He shrugged. "Just asking." In seconds, he had finished what was left of her lunch. She gathered he did everything the way he ate and wasn't much on wasting time.

Jack shook his head when Jenny brought up the importance of small talk. "Let's skip that."

"Are you going to skip dinner parties?"

"As many as I can," he said.

"There will be some you'll have to go to. You'll be expected to be a good conversationalist."

He leaned back in his chair, ignoring her. "How about some Courvoisier?"

"If you like. But I'd better stick with my wine."

"Oh, come on. It's free. You know as well as I do this lunch is going to be billed back to my firm." She smiled at his bluntness.

"And that's why I want to make sure you get your money's worth," she said, taking a deep breath. "So back to small talk. You could begin a conversation with how lovely the centerpiece is." He turned his thumb down on that. "Or how tasty the food is." He waved his hand from side to side. "Or," she said, trying to think of something that would appeal to him, "you could mention a good book you've read lately." He shook his head. "Or," she tried again, "a good play or movie you've seen."

"How about last night's boxing match?" His eyes twinkled with amusement.

She was about ready to wring his neck. "I don't think that's going to work." From his expression she could tell he didn't intend to take this seriously. She tried to think what would get through to him. "You're not being considerate of that refined lady—"

"Lady?" he interrupted her. She had finally caught his interest.

"Your dinner partner. The one who's had the good fortune to sit next to you. Or should I say misfortune?" She looked him straight in the eye. He laughed. "The woman next to you is going to be well read, well traveled, and interested in many things, like most of the women in Washington. But she's not going to be interested in talking about boxing."

"That's fine with me," he said. "I can't stand her type, anyway." He took a sip of his brandy.

Jenny sighed, not knowing what approach to follow next.

"You know," he said, checking his watch, "I like you. You're smart. But I am what I am.

It's too bad that my partners are so delicate they can't stomach anyone who doesn't look and act like them. What would the idiots do if I was an amputee? Expect me to grow another leg? No, I'm not changing for them."

"Even if it means not making as much money as you could?" she said, thinking that might get through to him.

"Don't worry," he said, his eyebrows arching. "I make more than enough. I'm good at what I do. That's all that counts in the real world." Leaning back in his chair, he studied her. "You look like you're doing all right for yourself. If you're interested in tax shelters, I've got a great deal for you."

"No, thanks."

"I know exactly what you mean. That's just how I feel about this deal too. No, thanks." It was a perfect understanding. They had come to a truce.

"You know, Jack, I like you the way you are." She smiled. "Tell your partners you're a hopeless case—there will be no charge."

Hetty had a glass of wine ready for Jenny when she walked in the door. "Happy birthday," she said, saluting Jenny with her sherry. "I suppose you're in a hurry to get ready for dinner with Steve."

"Yes. What's on your agenda for tonight?"

"George is taking me out for dinner to La Coquille."

"Fancy."

"He was hoping you'd join us, but I said you'd be tied up with Steve," Hetty said with a wink.

Jenny smiled, still unsure if she should risk tying herself up with Steve. "Perhaps I can join you and George some other time. But let it be at a less expensive restaurant, please."

"Oh, that doesn't matter to him. He's loaded. Plus, he's anxious to talk to you." Jenny saw a smile creep up on Hetty's face and a twinkle appear in her eye. "I think he wants to ask your permission to marry me."

"Already? You've just met."

Hetty laughed. "Just kidding. But we do like each other a lot." Jenny sensed that a wedding might not be far off, and that Hetty was trying to prepare her for it. "You'd really like him, Jenny."

"I'm sure I would."

Hetty asked Jenny how her day had gone. She always said Jenny's office stories were better than her daytime soaps. Hearing about Jack Ross brought tears of laughter to Hetty's eyes. "You've got to introduce me to your diamond-in-the-rough sometime," she said.

"Sorry, but I don't think I'll be seeing him again. We called it quits." Then Jenny told her how she couldn't convince Jack to change his image. "You know, he's right. Why should he have to change to accommodate people so narrow-minded that they can't associate with anyone the least bit different from themselves?"

"Jenny, that kind of thinking doesn't go along with the job you do."

"I know. But why change people when they're fine the way they are, like Jack Ross?" Jenny paused and looked off, then said, "And Steve."

"Look, you're not really changing Steve or anyone else. You're not that powerful—no one is. All you're paid to do is give people skills, nothing more, like a piano teacher. And what they do with those skills is their responsibility, not yours. So, don't be a worrying old hen. If they hadn't come to you, they would have gone to someone else in the business of making perfect people for perfect lives."

Jenny smiled, recalling her days with Vance. "Perfect people, perfect lives. I, of all people, should be aware that neither exists."

Chapter Seven

"*Bon soir,* Mr. Voight," the maître d' said, recognizing Steve as soon as he and Jenny entered the restaurant, one of the most expensive in Washington. He signaled to an older waiter, dressed in a tuxedo, who escorted them to the table Steve had reserved.

"I'm impressed," Jenny whispered to Steve as they walked, her arm in his. A few steps ahead the waiter busily clicked his fingers at the young busboys he passed. "You must come here often."

"Not really," he answered out of the side of his mouth. "He must have a good memory." Jenny knew the waiters in town had good memories for frequent guests and those whom they thought were important, but not for the average man on the street.

Steve recognized a man at a table they passed. The man rose to meet Steve's outstretched hand and said, "Good to see you."

That phrase grated on Jenny like chalk on

a blackboard. She had heard it over and over again. "Good to see you" was a catchall phrase. It covered all bases, something safe to say whether or not you had met the person before. Jenny doubted if the man had the foggiest idea who Steve was.

"I'll be just a minute," Steve said, excusing himself to Jenny, then asking the waiter to escort her to their table.

From where she sat, she could see that the man seemed impatient with Steve. About ten minutes later, Steve joined her, apologizing for the interruption. "Who is he?" Jenny asked.

"Head of one of the biggest farmers' groups in town. His name is Callahan. I've been trying to set a date with him for weeks. It's been hard to pin him down. No one around here has a minute to spare."

"I'm beginning to think that includes you too," Jenny said.

"I guess that's true until the bill gets settled. But for the rest of the night I'm all yours." He bent over and whispered in her ear, "Happy birthday, Jen."

"By the way, how did you know it was my birthday?"

"You told me."

"When?"

"Don't you remember the afternoon we met at Dumbarton Oaks?"

"Yes, very well."

"And when we were looking at the zodiac circle?"

"Yes."

"That was when you said your birthday was April twenty-eighth."

"Yes, I did. I had forgotten that." Jenny looked down as she recalled their romantic encounter in the gardens. She didn't want him to suspect the pleasant feeling it brought back to her.

"I didn't forget it." He took her hand.

"I know. Thank you for the perfume," she said, feeling his warm fingers wrap around hers. "How did you know that was the scent I wear? Or was it a coincidence you picked the right one?"

"No, it wasn't a coincidence."

"Don't tell me you sniffed all the bottles at the perfume counter, looking for it."

He laughed. "No. You told me."

"Again!"

"On our first date, at the café where we stopped for dessert. Remember, when I helped you put on your coat, I asked you what kind of perfume you were wearing?"

"No. But I remember your helping me with my coat." That night came back to her in a flash, and the way he had offered to pour cream into her coffee.

The waiter came with dinner menus. Steve urged her to choose from the more expensive dishes while he studied the wine list. He waited for her to decide before selecting a wine for their dinner. "An excellent choice, *monsieur,*" the wine steward said with a slight bow when Steve ordered a *Bâtard-Montrachet.*

Steve spread a wedge of toast with the caviar their waiter had brought as a compliment from the maître d', and offered it to Jenny. "How's Hetty doing?" he asked.

Jenny told Steve about Hetty's increasing interest in George Mahoney. "They're out almost every day—"

"Hey, Steve," a heavily made-up, long-haired blonde, wearing a gold-lame slip of a dress, called out to Steve.

"Candy Carson," he said, getting up to greet her.

"Good to see you," she said.

Great! Another one from the Hill Jenny thought as Candy and her escort came over.

"Hey, why don't we eat together?" Candy suggested, much to Jenny's chagrin. "Your table is big enough."

Steve looked at Jenny, hesitating to agree. Jenny sensed his mixed emotions and gathered Candy might be someone influential. She didn't want to spoil his chances. So, trying to sound enthusiastic, she said, "That sounds like a lovely idea." Steve smiled at her and squeezed her hand. But Jenny couldn't help wishing he had come up with an excuse not to have Candy around.

Before sitting down, Candy introduced her companion, Stewart Pierce, to them, referring to him as her "current pal." Stewart was a lawyer with one of Washington's largest law firms. "I got him his job," Candy said. "He's up for partner this year." She gave him a pinch under his chin. "I sure got them a good catch." He smiled and gave Jenny a flirting wink when Candy wasn't looking.

The dinners Steve and Jenny had ordered were brought to their table. Candy and Stewart hurried to order from their menus, urging Steve and Jenny to start eating. But Steve and Jenny politely waited.

Candy told Jenny that she was a lobbyist, representing most of the clothing manufacturers in the United States. "As Steve knows, I have great connections in Washington," she said. Then she went on extensively about how she had slowed down the investigations that were being done concerning illegal aliens employed in the garment district.

Jenny was curious about how much Candy really had to do with that. She remembered reading in the papers, a couple of years ago, about raids on various factories and arrests of illegal aliens. Now it seemed to be a dead issue. Maybe Candy Carson was smarter than she looked.

By the time Candy and Stewart were served, the cream sauce on Jenny's veal was beginning to gel around the colorful assortment of julienne vegetables. Jenny took her first bite. It didn't taste very good cold, and the evening slid downhill from there.

It seemed like an eternity to Jenny before their after-dinner coffee was served. She was afraid Steve might pick up the check, grateful for all the valuable information Candy had given him. Actually, she suspected that was exactly what Candy had in mind. Candy had monopolized Steve's ear, explaining her business methods to him. She was especially proud of the tactics she had devised to minimize costs.

Jenny wasn't sure if it was her bored look or his watch that told Steve it was time to go. But she was glad when he asked for the check. Candy argued, but not too strongly, to split the bill when Steve insisted on paying for all four of them. Jenny smiled to herself, thinking, *She's really something.*

"Sorry, Jen," Steve said outside, waiting for the valet to bring his car. "I shouldn't have let them join us."

"I suppose it would have been awkward to refuse," she said, trying to be a good sport.

Opening the car door for her, he said, more to himself than to her, "So little time, so much to do." He turned the ignition and looked at her. "I wanted to make this evening a perfect birthday celebration for you. So far, I'm bombing on that." She smiled at him. "Are you willing to try someplace else?"

"Where?" she asked.

"The boat. Okay?" he asked, as if she might prefer not to go.

"That sounds like a lovely idea," she said in the same tone she had used earlier when Candy suggested they all eat dinner together. Steve laughed, appreciating her little quip. Jenny looked up at him and smiled. "But this time I mean it."

Steve switched on the inside lights of the houseboat. Everything looked very orderly and neat, suggesting to Jenny that Steve hadn't been home very much. "How about some coffee?" he asked, helping her take off her white mohair spring coat.

"You've just read my mind."

He smiled. "I wish I could." He hesitated as if he was about to kiss her, then smiled again and headed for the kitchen.

Jenny kicked off her high heels and settled down on the couch as Steve carried over two mugs in one hand and a full coffeepot in the other. He sat beside her and loosened his tie. Putting his feet up on the glass coffee table, he coaxed her head onto his shoulder. She let herself rest against his body as he stroked her hair. Outside, she could see the wavy reflection of the moon, fluorescent against the darkness of the river.

They listened to soft music and the gentle night waves. He told her how bad the farmers' situation was back home. She was glad he could unburden himself to her. Later they spoke freely of little inconsequential thoughts that came and passed quickly through their minds. "Did you catch the name of the firm Candy's friend is with?"…"I hear a fog horn"…"Is that the Big Dipper up there?" She felt so relaxed with him. She had never felt that relaxed with a man.

She turned to look at him; his loving eyes were already on her. He drew her closer to him. His fingers slid through her hair as his mouth met hers. "Oh, Jen," he whispered through his kiss. "I love you so much."

Jenny pulled away and covered her ears. "Please, don't say that!" she cried.

"Why?" He held her tight so she couldn't turn away from him. "Why, Jen?"

Grabbing his shirt in frustration, Jenny asked, "Why can't we leave it simple and uncomplicated?"

"Because my feelings for you are not simple and uncomplicated. There's something between us. Don't you feel it?"

She lowered her head and closed her eyes. She couldn't look at his pleading cycs, nor dare admit to him or even to herself that she wanted his love. "You don't understand. It's not hard for you to love again. All you're looking for is another chance to be happy. I had that chance once, and it almost destroyed me." She looked up and saw his puzzled concern. Could he possibly understand what she was about to say? "You know your friend Tillie?" she asked.

"The one who has a nervous breakdown every time she dates?"

Jenny nodded. "I'm like Tillie." He looked confused. "I can't handle any involvement with men. My nerves fall apart."

He lifted her face toward him. His kiss was strong, filled with yearning. Drawing his lips away, he searched her eyes and asked, "Did that upset you?"

"No." She couldn't help smiling. In fact, it had felt very good. There was no tightening of her stomach, but would that return if their relationship were more serious?

Steve gently squeezed her close. "See? Then everything is okay. There's nothing to worry about."

"It's not that easy." Jenny pushed him away, annoyed that he was taking this so lightly. He needed to know about Vance in order to understand.

She told him how she had met Vance when he came out to buy a neighbor's farm for investment purposes. She had just graduated from college. He had all the elegance and grace of the upper-crust family he had been born into. He was truly a Prince Charming who swept her off her feet. She had loved everything about him and had wanted to be just like him and his family. That was where her problems had begun.

"I tried to ignore his friends' whispers about Vance and the farmer's daughter," Jenny said. "But I couldn't help feeling like a curiosity, a new gadget for them to play with. I just didn't know how to act with them. They were so different from the people I knew."

Steve held her closer, easing the pain of her rising memories and freeing her to talk on. "I depended on Vance not to let me make a mistake. I used him as my instant gauge. A smile from him meant I was doing fine, and a frown meant I was not. I was like a child looking up to a father, and he was happy playing that role." Jenny shook her head. "I did everything I could to be like them. I tried so hard to please him. But in doing so, I was losing myself."

She told Steve how she began to resent Vance's smiles and frowns. "I started looking inward to my values and not those of others. When I met Vance, I wanted to be taken care of. But somehow nature pushes us to grow up and to want to take care of ourselves. During the time we dated, by seeing his friends and how they lived, I came to realize that self-esteem comes from one's self, not from the clothes one wears or from a husband or a job. I grew up. I was ready to be a wife and wanted a husband, not a father." Jenny shrugged as she looked at Steve.

"He wanted a daughter, not a wife?" She nodded. "I was so afraid of what our marriage would be like. I felt the old Jenny would never measure up. She would have to die so a new Jenny could be born. But I had no idea who the Jenny I would have to be was. I was really scared.

"My nerves just went out of control. I couldn't eat or sleep. By the time our wedding day came, I was trembling all over and couldn't move out of bed. Vance said it was just prenuptial nerves. He thought everything would be okay after the wedding."

"Didn't you tell him why you were afraid?" "It was easy to talk to him about fun things but not about things like that. He'd say something like 'Oh, Jennifer,'—he always called me Jennifer—'you're being a silly little thing.' And that was it. His wall would go up, and I could never break through it."

Gently Steve caressed her face and bent down to her lips. His kiss was strong and binding, as if he wanted to heal her pain. She fought the power she knew it could have over her and felt him withdraw. He held her face between his hands so he could look into her eyes and she could see his. "You know that wall you were just talking about?" he asked. She nodded, realizing his frustration. "You're putting it up between us. I can feel it." Jenny closed her eyes so she couldn't see his hurt.

"Why, Jen?" he asked, stroking her cheek. "What are you afraid of?"

"Of love," she whispered, feeling a tear fall from the corner of her eye.

"Jen, this is so right. Can't you believe it?" She shook her head. She felt his breath close to her face. She opened her eyes and saw his lips drawing toward her as he said, "I'm going to break through that wall." She felt his whole body and soul crying out to her through his kiss, and she tightened every muscle she could to stop herself from answering him the way she wanted to. If she would ever let herself love again, he would be the one. But she wasn't willing to commit herself, to believe it could work for her.

He pulled away, shaking his head. "That's a mighty thick wall," he said with a half smile. Jenny tried to smile back. "I hope I can find a crack in it," he said firmly, "before one of us dies."

Between Mary and Chip, he knew all too well the brevity of life. He was reminding her of that. Jenny fully grasped the message he wanted to convey. The thought of his ever dying disturbed her more than she wanted it to.

Chapter Eight

"You're rather cheery this morning," Jenny said to Hetty, who was fluttering around and humming to herself.

"I am—I went dancing with George last night," Hetty sang in response.

"Aren't you getting tired of all this togetherness?"

"No, it's just like Nathan. I could have been with him every minute of the day, and that wouldn't have been enough."

Jenny knew about Nathan. Hetty spoke of him often as if it had been only yesterday, and not almost seventy years ago, when they met. "Our wedding night was a night to last me a lifetime," Hetty had said. A week later he was called into the Service. He was killed overseas. Though she had many suitors after Nathan, Hetty never remarried.

"Nathan was the best. It's been downhill ever since," Hetty said, referring to the men she had dated.

"How could you stand it?"

"Oh, I met some nice men. But never anyone like Nathan. I suppose we never get over our first love. I guess that's the curse of being a woman."

"You're lucky to have known such a love once," Jenny said wistfully. Unrest among the farmers had called Steve back home again. He had already been gone several weeks. She missed him a lot, and found herself acquiescing to his wanting to chip at that wall of hers.

"And I think I've lucked out again," Hetty said, a smile creeping out from the corners of her mouth.

"You mean George?"

Hetty nodded, smoothing out an embroidered doily under a silver tea set. "I've got to be hurrying along. George is taking me out for lunch."

"Where do you get all your energy?"

"Make hay while the sun shines, as they say! Time's running out on us." She looked scoldingly at Jenny. "Young lady, you should be making hay with Steve, you know."

Jenny laughed. "Well, you'd be pleased to know that's what I'm about to do. Steve called last night and invited me to visit the haystacks."

"He did?"

"Not exactly. He didn't specify haystacks, but he wants me to come out."

"You're going, of course?"

"Yes, but only for a long weekend. There's too much going on here for me to be away longer. Besides, he has his hands full too, trying to calm down the farmers."

"What's up?" Hetty asked, always interested in happenings in the world.

"They're getting pretty restless, and there's some talk about organizing a nationwide strike."

"A strike! I can't imagine that happening. They're too independent."

"But they're plenty mad. That's doing a good job of uniting them. Soon, I'll be finding out first hand what it's all about." Jenny said. She sighed.

"Why the sad face?" Hetty asked.

"I'm a little nervous about how this is going to work out. I feel that I'm risking a lot."

"Risking a chance to love? That's not a lot," Hetty said dreamily, and Jenny sensed she wanted to be with George.

"I just don't know how I'll cope," Jenny told her. "It's hard loving someone who's on the run all the time."

Hetty shrugged. "It can be, but you said Steve's nice."

"Yes, he is."

"Then tough it out. It's pretty hard finding a nice man among all the egotists in this town."

* * *

Jenny felt very tense during her flight, not because of the plane ride, but because of the risk she was taking. Everyone had called her "not the marrying kind." Even her mother had said so too. Was she too selfish to live with a man? Other women gave up everything for the men they loved. But she couldn't. She couldn't do it for Vance; she couldn't do it for any man, no matter what. Did that make her "not the marrying kind"? Perhaps it did, if it meant she would have to lose herself to the very man she loved.

Already, she felt she had gotten a taste of what that could be like with Steve. They had argued when he called to ask her to come to the farm. He hadn't given her much notice. He wanted her to come for a week, but rescheduling appointments for that long a time, some of them already pressing, was impossible. "I just can't," she had told Steve.

"You're sure?"

"Yes."

"I miss you a lot," Steve had said.

"But not enough to come back," had slipped out of Jenny's mouth before she could catch herself.

"Jen, I could say the same about you—not enough to come here." He was right, and she had been angry with herself for saying what she had. If this was a taste of what juggling their careers and their relationship was going to be like, she wasn't handling it very well.

"Maybe I could get away for a long weekend," she had said.

"That would be great if you could." She could tell even over the phone that he really wanted her with him. But as the plane landed, she worried where all this was heading, and hoped, for her, that it wouldn't be a dead end.

Steve was at the airport to meet her. The sight of him lifted all her misgivings. He was watching for her as she came through the gate. His tall figure was easy to spot in the crowd, and a big smile broke out on his face the second her waving caught his attention. His smile was all for her, and his arms opened wide as she ran up to him. He hugged her tight, and she felt she was home where she belonged. Gone was the subtle emptiness she had felt while he was away, a sense of things just not being quite right. She felt whole again, completely intact.

She teased him about the plaid shirt, dungarees, and fancy leather boots he was wearing. "I'm not sure how that would go over back in Washington."

Steve smiled. "We're not in Washington, and I think you're going to find it a pleasant change."

"It doesn't look like you're working any less, though. You look tired."

"I guess I am. I've been listening to a lot of

people talk about their problems. But I'll rest better now that you're with me."

"I'm sorry it can't be for longer."

"Me too. But I'm glad you're here, anyway." Jenny had explained to Steve before she left that the long weekend she had planned had to be shortened. Anna had to make another trip to the Middle East, and Jenny was carrying a double load. She had to be back at the office on Monday.

During the two-hour drive from the airport to Steve's farm, Steve told her about his morning meeting with some county commissioners and other representatives.

"You met on Saturday?" she said, surprised.

"They're meeting seven days a week," Steve said, rubbing his forehead. He looked worn out. He told Jenny about the strike the farmers were planning. "I don't think it will really come to pass. There are too many who feel it's only going to create more bitterness. And I agree. But it's discussed a lot." He talked about those working with him, almost one-third women, some of whom were political appointees.

That surprised Jenny. In her youth, most women had spent their time in the kitchen, canning and baking. She remembered them talking mostly about recipes and raising children. But Jenny was well aware that times had changed. For one thing, the roaming farmhands were gone. And if they were still around, the money just wasn't there anymore to hire them. Farmers' wives were riding tractors alongside their husbands, many finding work in town to make ends meet. They did what they had to do. They came from pioneer stock, and it was in their blood not to give up. Their homesteading ancestors had needed a help-mate as much, if not more, than they needed a wife, and had chosen their spouses well. It was character they sought, not delicate features, and above all strength—the strength and courage needed to survive the frontier wilderness.

From what Steve said, the women working with him exhibited that same strength. Along with the men, they had kept abreast of what was happening in Washington and were fully aware and appreciative of the progress Steve had made. They were up to date on the implications of the new tax bill for farmers and the consequences of the increasing trade deficit.

As Steve went into more detail about what had been discussed, Jenny became bothered that some of the positions he took seemed opposed to those of the farmers. When she told him that, he smiled, not angered or taking offense. With him, she could feel free to speak her mind without feeling as if she were walking on eggs. She had felt this way with Vance, who was so quick to take what she said the wrong way.

"I have to play the devil's advocate," Steve said. "Sometimes the farmers are all too quick to close their ears to the other guy's argument and hear only what they want to hear. They need to know that an aging widow living on Social Security is far from sympathetic to their cause when, at least, they have a farm to lose, whereas she has nothing. She's exhausted her savings and can hardly afford a loaf of bread, and is scared to death over the thought of food prices going up. But they don't want to hear that. Or that they're not the only ones hurting, that factories are closing down and a lot of people are out of work."

It was dusk when Steve turned off onto the dirt road leading to his home. Jenny had forgotten how spacious the Midwest was. You could drive for miles with fields on either side without passing another car or house.

She walked up to the front porch that wrapped around the two-story house. Inside, the honey tones of the oak floors and doors and the heirloom furnishings gave a warmth and coziness to the large rooms. Jenny picked up an oval frame containing an old photo of a couple with two small children on their laps. The resemblance was striking, but they seemed too old to be Steve's parents. "Who are they?" she asked.

Steve leaned over her shoulder and looked fondly at the picture. "My folks. That's Kathy and that's me."

"Your parents?"

"Yes. They thought they couldn't have any children. Kathy and I were their packages from heaven, as they said, that arrived a little late but were worth the wait." He smiled.

Jenny smiled too, looking at a young Steve. "It must have been difficult for you at times, having parents older than those of your friends," Jenny said.

"No, not at all. They spoiled us terribly. Not materially; there wasn't enough for that. But they weren't very strict with us. I always remember them smiling. They said Kathy and I made them smile." Steve spoke warmly, and his willingness to be so open about himself pleased her. "I can't recall them ever raising their voices at us."

"I think you had the kind of parents kids dream of."

Steve smiled as he took the picture from Jenny so he could hold it in his hands. "Kathy and I knew we did. That's why their age never bothered us except in that it didn't give them very much time to be with us. They got to see us both grown and married. But soon after Kathy married Chip, they died within a year of each other. They were very close. I guess it was better for them that way."

For them, Jenny thought, *but not for Steve.* She sensed he missed them, and after what he had told her, she could understand why. She, too, felt a loss—the loss of never having the chance to know them.

"I bet they would be real proud to see you now," she said, "wrapping Washington around your little finger."

Steve laughed. "If only I could really do that." He picked up Jenny's bag. "Come on, you probably want to unpack and get into some comfortable clothes."

Steve showed Jenny to a room at the top of the stairs. It was small, but bright and airy, and reminded Jenny of the bedroom she had shared with her sister back on the farm. "Kathy stopped by and fixed it up for you before she left."

"Left?"

Steve nodded. "She's spending some time with Chip's family."

"Oh, I was really looking forward to meeting her."

"She wanted to meet you too. But Chip's mother asked her to come. His dad is still pretty down, and she's worried about him. He's very fond of Kathy, and she thought a visit from Kathy might cheer him up."

"Do you think she's ready to handle the burden of someone else's grief too?"

"I think so. It was her decision to go. Each

day it seems that I'm finding out more and more how strong she really is. You'll get to meet her soon. I'm bringing her back to Washington with me." Steve left Jenny to unpack and went downstairs to fix some dinner.

Jenny was slipping into a jogging suit when she got a whiff of something cooking. Downstairs she found Steve standing over a stove, stirring a pot of beef stew. "Boy, does that smell good," she said. "You sure did whip that up fast."

Steve smiled. "Only reheating it. It was there when I opened the refrigerator."

"Just like magic."

"Not quite." Steve said, chuckling. "I suspect Norman brought it over."

"Who's Norman?"

"He's got the farm next to us." He ladled some stew into a bowl for Jenny. "Here, have a taste."

"Mmm, that's good. Norman's a good cook."

Steve laughed. "Norman wouldn't be caught dead in the kitchen. His wife does all the cooking. The vegetables are fresh from her garden."

"It sure was nice of them to bring this over. Nice and neighborly," she said as they sat down at the table.

"Well, that's how it is out here."

"It's so quiet and peaceful too," Jenny said, then laughed at herself. "I'm not used to this much peace and quiet. I don't know if I could take this kind of life."

Steve smiled. "It's a good life, but not without its worries." He looked out the window over the kitchen sink to the newly planted wheat field stretching out for miles under the rosy glow of the setting sun. "But working out here, you're your own man. God's your only boss."

"Do you miss it?"

"At times, especially on the days when I've been run ragged and feel I've accomplished nothing. But I'm geared up for a different kind of life now. Going back to farming would be an adjustment."

"Then you don't think you ever will?"

"I don't know. Right now I like what I'm doing in Washington. I'm having a lot of interesting experiences." He smiled. "And I never would have met you if I had stayed here."

Jenny smiled back, glad, too, that he had left the farm.

Steve offered to refill her plate.

"No, thanks. I've got some extra pounds to lose." Business lunches and dinners always played havoc with her diets.

"What extra pounds? I like you just the way you are." Jenny smiled, glad he did. She thought back to her time with Vance, when she was a lot thinner. All the women in his circle worked out at a health spa at least an hour a day to stay a size six, or at most eight. If you became a size ten, you were practically ostracized. The women had the same beautiful bodies, same version of the same hairdo done by the same currently "in" hairstylist, same gorgeous tans, same designer fashions. It was all the *same*. No contrasts to stimulate one's senses, no differences to stir one's passions, no surprises to spark one's days. She was glad to be out of it and twenty pounds heavier.

Steve leaned back and, imitating an English gentleman, said, "Shall we repair to the living room, my lady?" He took Jenny's hand and guided her over to the couch. "You're good for me," he said, putting his arms around her. "I haven't felt this relaxed since I was last with you."

"You're good for me too."

"We could be so good for each other." His fingers gently stroked her cheeks and then the edge of her lips. The pleasure of his closeness only made her realize more that the wall she had built around her wasn't on a very sound foundation. She felt so vulnerable—so very vulnerable to being hurt again.

His eyes focused on her lips as he bent toward her mouth. It was a questioning yet tender kiss. When she didn't resist as she had before, his kiss grew stronger. All his love for her poured forth. And the doors of her heart split open, breaking down her wall, releasing her love for him.

Then she felt him take a deep breath and draw away. "Thank heaven," she heard him say, holding her tight. She drew back enough to look into his eyes and saw sheer joy. And her love cried out to him.

"I love you so much," he said, his dark, clear eyes looking into hers, "it hurts."

"I love you too," she said, bringing his lips again to hers. Just as they touched, the phone rang. Steve answered. His face blanched. Something awful must have happened. Jenny listened to Steve reassure the woman on the phone. "Don't worry, Molly," he said, calmly. "I'll be right over. He's probably just gone someplace to cool off."

Steve put his hand over the receiver. Contrary to his tone of voice with Molly, he did look worried. He quickly explained that Molly's husband had walked out on her. He was another financially troubled farmer, and Molly was worried sick over him. "I've got to go," he said apologetically to Jenny.

"I understand."

Steve handed Jenny the phone, asking her to talk a little longer with Molly until he arrived. Jenny introduced herself to Molly as a friend of Steve's. The woman was so upset that Jenny could barely understand what she was trying to say. She kept on repeating, "My husband hit me. He never hit me before." Then she cried in desperation, "I don't know what to do."

Jenny tried to calm her. The woman had gotten a job delivering mail to help out with their money problems. She said her husband had always been so good to her and the children. She was frantic. He had run out the door and driven off in the pickup as soon as he realized what he had done. He had been gone several hours. She had no idea where he was. Jenny tried to encourage Molly not to think the worst. But she couldn't help thinking of Steve's brother-in-law, and she knew what Molly feared.

It seemed like forever before Steve got on the line to say he was at Molly's. He told Jenny not to wait up for him; he didn't know when he would get back. It was midnight when Jenny felt calmed down enough to go to bed. Steve still hadn't returned.

The next morning, Jenny found a note from Steve slipped under her bedroom door, saying that he got home very late last night. Jenny fixed herself some eggs and coffee, not bothering to call Steve for breakfast. After all he'd been through, he deserved some rest.

She took her second cup of coffee out to the porch. It was nice to sit in the double swing and not have to rush off. She could hear the melodic creak of the windmill off in the distance by the woodshed, and watched a lark dart among the trees shading the side of the house. The morning passed quickly.

Hearing the putter of a tractor around the side of the barn, she got up to see who it was. A middle-aged man in dusty coveralls was riding down the pasture road. He waved and pulled up near her.

"Howdy," he said, removing his straw hat. "You must be Jenny Foster." Jenny nodded. "I'm Norman Swanson. I live—"

"Oh, you're the one who brought the stew. We sure enjoyed it," Jenny said, shouting over the noise of the motor.

"Glad you did." He smiled, his teeth shining white against his weathered tan. "Are you going to be with us for a while?"

"No. I've got a plane to catch this afternoon."

"That's too bad." He parked the tractor by the side of the barn and came over to her. "Steve around?"

"He's sleeping. There was trouble at Molly's last night."

"Yep. I heard what happened." Jenny was surprised he knew. "News travels fast around here," he said, answering her unspoken question.

"Do you know if they found him?"

"Haven't heard anything yet. It's good Steve went over. Steve's quite a guy. There's none like him. I'd probably have been another one who'd put a noose around my neck if it weren't for him." Jenny cringed, thinking Molly's husband might have done just that.

Norman wiped his brow with the brim of his hat. "The bank was on my back," he said, "and I had to sell off most of my land to get any credit with them. Steve bought a good half of what was auctioned off." Norman shook his head. "He bid real high, and he could have gotten it for a lot less than he paid. That was a big break for me—it put some cash back into my pockets. And then he turns around and says he doesn't have the time to farm it—he wants me to take care of it. Then he tells me to keep the crops because he doesn't need them." Norman started to walk over to his pickup, which was parked by the side of the road.

Jenny followed him. "I'm glad to hear he's helped you out."

"I'm not the only one. Since he's been in Washington and hasn't the time to farm, he's been renting out sections of his farm to guys like me at the cheapest rate around. He sure could earn a lot more if he wanted to. He doesn't suffer any from greed."

"Maybe he feels he has enough."

Norman shrugged. "Guess so. He sure isn't making much off the land he bought from me."

"Well, at least you're farming it."

Norman turned toward her and smiled. "Steve says he wants to keep it plowed because it's a good investment."

"Is it?"

He shrugged. "I'm not sure. But he does have a potential buyer."

"Who?"

"Me. Thanks to him, someday I'll have enough money saved up to buy back my land. And knowing Steve, the price will be more than fair."

It was almost noon when Steve awoke, just about in time to take Jenny to the airport. He looked like he hadn't slept enough. She felt awful making him face the long drive to the airport and back home again. "Is there another way I can get there?" she asked.

"Nothing doing. I haven't seen enough of you as it is. A few more hours together in the car will more than make up for the ride back. I'm sorry, Jen. I didn't need to bring you out here to be alone."

"You couldn't help it. How can you cope with all these problems? I could hardly bear to listen to Molly on the phone."

"I don't know. But when they call on me, I can't refuse. We're all in this little world together—in good times and in bad."

Jenny thought how right Norman was when he said Steve was quite a guy. He wasn't one to walk out on trouble, and he wouldn't be one to walk out on her. She felt lucky to be loving him, and more confident that she wouldn't turn into a Tillie and he wouldn't turn into a Vance.

Chapter Nine

Gladys looked worried when Jenny came into the office Monday morning.

"What's wrong?" Jenny asked.

"Anna's back from the Middle East. She said she got in last night."

"And…."

"That's all," Gladys said. "She went into her office and closed the door."

Hearing that alarmed Jenny—Anna never closed the door to her office.

Jenny knocked on Anna's door, but Anna didn't answer. She opened the door a crack and thought she heard sobbing. She pushed the door further open, and found Anna with her head bent over her arms on her desk. Quietly, Jenny closed the door behind her. Anna looked up—her face was streaked with tears and runny makeup.

"What's the matter?" Jenny asked, very concerned. She had never seen her this way. Anna was always upbeat, always smiling.

"Joe wants a divorce."

"I can't believe that."

"I can't believe it either."

"What happened?"

"I'm not sure. He says he doesn't like being left alone. I'm traveling so much."

"But how about all the times he left you alone when he was on diplomatic missions?"

"I know. I reminded him about that. I told him that the only reason I started this business was to fill my empty hours while he was busy working his head off."

"Is there another woman?"

"I don't know. He says there isn't."

"Anna, I don't understand. I always thought you and Joe had a perfect marriage."

"So did I. I guess it *was* perfect when I stayed home and cooked for him and ironed his shirts and took care of the kids. It's amazing how we can fool ourselves into thinking we're really in love."

"If you two aren't, I don't know who is."

"I don't know either. I feel like the whole world's been turned upside down. I've been racking my brains, trying to find out what went wrong. Looking back, I can see signals that I ignored or passed over. There were indications that something was going wrong. It's so obvious now, but it wasn't then. It's amazing how blind love can be."

"But you've been together so long. How many years is it now?"

"Almost thirty."

"I can't believe that after all that time, it can be anything too serious. Have you thought of marriage counseling?"

"Yes, and I've suggested it to Joe. But he won't consider it."

"Why?"

"He said it's too late. He said we've worked ourselves out of each other's lives. Maybe he's right." Anna put her head back down.

"Is there anything I can do?"

"No, just let me rest. My head feels like a sledgehammer went through it."

Jenny went back to her office. Seeing what was happening to Anna and Joe, whose marriage she had always thought of as solid, made her doubts return. Perhaps letting herself fall in love with Steve was a mistake. Yet, at the same time, she wished he were near so she could touch him, rest her head against his shoulder, find comfort in him.

The phone rang, startling her. Steve was calling from the farm to see how she was doing. "Did they find Molly's husband?" Jenny asked him.

"Yes, dead drunk in a gully by the road. His truck was at the bar. Looks like he forgot he had driven there and had started walking home. It's a happier ending than most."

"What's going to happen now?"

"He's admitted he needs help. That's a hard thing for a farmer to do. Probably explains why he got good and drunk. He said he loves Molly. She's the last one in the world he'd want to hurt. It scared him that he had lashed out at her that way. They're going into therapy together."

"And how about Kathy? Have you heard from her?"

"She's okay but wants to stay on a little longer with Chip's family. I guess she won't be coming back with me."

"That's too bad. I really am eager to meet her."

"Oh, you will. She promised me she'd come pretty soon. I expect to be tied up with work when I get back. So, it's probably for the best. I wouldn't have much time to spend with her, anyway." He paused, then said, "Jen?"

"Yes."

"I've been missing you. It's not the same without you."

She wanted to tell him about Anna, to hear him say it couldn't happen to them. But before she had the chance, he said he had to run. He had another meeting to go to. So she postponed telling him what was on her mind until the next time he called.

But the chance to tell him about Anna never came. He called often enough during the remaining weeks he was away, but was always in a rush. Even though his calls were short, she looked forward to them. But living from one call to the next and hanging up without much time to talk was frustrating. Their hurried conversations became so superficial that Jenny wondered if they were really worth the bother. Yet, she knew they were—at least she got to hear his voice.

Things didn't get better after he was back in Washington. She gave up sharing her concerns with him. Every minute Steve had was spent lobbying congressmen and senators to vote for continued farm subsidies, and coordinating his efforts with those of other farm representatives. He still called to see how she was. But their planned get-togethers for lunch or dinner were always canceled for one reason or another.

"Don't go blaming yourself because you can't always be available for him, when you've got business appointments that can't and shouldn't be changed," Hetty said, having listened with guarded sympathy to Jenny's disappointment over another missed chance to be with Steve. "It's not entirely your fault, you know. How can he expect a busy woman like you to work your life around the couple of hours he's free, and on no more than a moment's notice?"

Jenny smiled. Hetty's reasoning had somewhat absolved her guilt. She took a sip of her wine. "Anything new with you?"

"I'm going out with George tonight."

Jenny laughed. "That's not new. You've been going out every day for weeks on end. Hasn't all this togetherness gotten to you yet?"

"No. In fact we're thinking of getting married and making it permanent."

Hetty had hinted that marriage might be coming, but Jenny never really took her seriously. "Isn't it kind of soon?" she asked.

Hetty laughed. "At our age, nothing's too soon."

"Have you already set a date?"

"Yes. I'm going to be a June bride," Hetty said, smiling from ear to ear.

"And you really love him?" Hetty nodded, her eyes twinkling with new life. "More than Nathan Taylor?"

The twinkle in Hetty's eyes ceased, her smile dropped for a split second, then reappeared. "As much."

Jenny knew that was enough. "June is only a month off," she said, seeing Hetty glow at the thought. "That doesn't give you much time to plan a wedding."

"It's not going to be much. Neither of us has any close family left, and most of our friends haven't stuck around as long as we have. We're just inviting you and George's nephew."

"The one he answered your personal-column ad for?"

"Yes. I guess you two are going to meet after all," Hetty said with a mischievous grin. "And, of course, your Mr. Voight will be included."

"Can I buy you a peignoir set?" Jenny asked.

"Of course. We're not *that* old!" Hetty leaned over to Jenny. "You know the saying 'Youth is wasted on the young'? It's true!" Hetty said, patting Jenny's hand. "And you know why?" Jenny shook her head, marveling at Hetty's youthful enthusiasm. "Because the young have a future. They have a tomorrow to try to make things better. We don't. They never think that this is the last time they'll ever be together. We do. And so we take our time, savor each kiss, each touch. Believe me, when this may be your last chance to love, you're not in a hurry for it to end."

During the next couple of weeks Jenny and Steve managed to squeeze in a few dates, if they could be called that. They met for a couple of hours on a Sunday afternoon at the National Gallery, near Steve's office. But Steve had to get back for an appointment with Jim Watson. They barely had enough time to share an old-fashioned banana split. Saying good-bye outside his office building, he leaned over and kissed her lightly on her lips and said, "Just being with you makes me so happy. It's all I want."

"Too bad your busy schedule doesn't allow for that."

"I know," he said, catching her slightly sarcastic tone. "Things are taking a lot longer on the Hill than I ever thought they would."

"That's the efficiency of our bureaucracy working."

"Unfortunately, it's costing me a lot." She was confused as to what he meant, and it must have shown in her expression. "It's costing me my time with you," he explained with a gentle kiss, then left to go back to work.

Jenny felt so alone. She tried to understand. She knew Steve was under a lot of pressure, and she knew very well what that was like. She had known days when she wanted to scream with frustration because twenty-four hours were barely enough to finish all that needed to be done. The farmers' bill would come to a vote soon, he had said, then they would have more time to be together. But it seemed like it was taking so long.

Then she received two free tickets for her and Steve from Mrs. Michel, the ambassador's wife. She had arranged for musicians from her Caribbean island to give a concert in Washington. Mrs. Michel had been following Jenny's advice well. Jenny had been reading a lot about her in the society columns. Evidently, Mrs. Michel was becoming quite a celebrity around town.

But at the last minute, Steve had to cancel out on her. Disappointed, Jenny invited Gladys to accompany her. After the performance, Mrs. Michel invited them back to the embassy for a private party. Gladys was all eyes and was thrilled to be meeting so many different people. This international side of Washington had never been opened to her before. Her delight helped ease Jenny's bitterness over having to ask someone to take Steve's place.

Another time Jenny joined Steve at a reception that he and an agricultural association were sponsoring. But so many people were vying for Steve's attention that she felt more in the way than anything else. The evening dragged on. She had had a very busy day at work and was exhausted. She collared Steve and told him she had an early appointment tomorrow and really should be going home.

"Oh, Jen, I can't leave now. I've got to wait until everyone is gone and the place is in order."

Jenny looked around. There were still a lot of guests hanging around the banquet room, laughing and looking as if they were having a good time. They didn't seem to be in any hurry to leave. "Don't worry, I'll take a cab," she said, too tired to wait.

"No, don't do that." He looked torn about

sending her home alone, and seemed to be thinking of something he could do. "At least let me have my chauffeur take you home."

Jenny sank down into the cushy seat in the back of the limousine Steve had rented to bring some congressmen over from the Hill. She found herself on the verge of tears. It was so childish to feel this way, not at all what she expected of herself. He had work to do. She couldn't expect him to stay by her side all the time. Besides, she couldn't always be accessible to him, either. She had a job too. But no matter how she tried, she could not rationalize away the hurt she felt.

Chapter Ten

Jenny thumbed through the files of the day's clients, having trouble concentrating on them. Again she told herself, for the umpteenth time, that Steve had a job to do and she should understand. She slammed the file shut. *I've got to stop letting my moods depend on Steve,* she thought. But no matter how she tried she could not chase away that nagging longing to see him. Without Steve, she felt so hollow, so empty. Not even her work could fill that void. How much better her life had been when it was uncomplicated by love! If not better, at least it was easier. Just at that moment, Anna barged in.

"You look like you're ready to spit in the devil's eye," Jenny said.

"I am, especially if his name is Joe," Anna said, collapsing into a chair.

'Trouble with the divorce agreement?"

Anna nodded. "You wouldn't believe what he wants to give me. Zip!"

'That's impossible."

"I know, and my lawyer won't let him get away with it. But I'm afraid we're going to have to go to court to get this thing settled. The amicable settlement he wanted is rapidly going down the drain."

"But why is Joe being so stingy, especially since he's the one who wants the divorce?"

"I don't have the slightest idea. You know," Anna said, "I'm beginning to wonder who I loved all these years. The side of him I'm seeing now is not the Joe I loved. I'm starting to wonder if the Joe I loved ever really existed. And if maybe this *is* the real Joe." She smiled regretfully. "They're not kidding when they say 'Love is blind.' "

"Well, anger has a way of bringing out the worst in us—and something seems to be making Joe very angry."

"Yeah, that I exist. That he can't just walk away with his pockets full."

"There's got to be more to it than that."

"Yes, and I'm seeing things in a clearer light now. Things that happened even before money issues came up, things that go back to the early part of our marriage. Things he said that I passed off, thinking he really didn't mean it. I'd blame it on the bad day he had or find some other excuse. I realize now that the marriage I thought I had was only a self-deception on my part. It was all a lie. That's what hurts the most."

Jenny left Anna to her thoughts. Anna was too upset to reason with any further. All Jenny could do was listen. It was healthy for Anna to vent her feelings. After a few minutes of reflection, Anna said, "Gladys told me that you've been putting in a lot of long nights."

"I thought I'd try putting together some new ideas we might want to pursue."

"Fine. But there's no need to cut into your personal life for that."

"I don't have much else to do."

"What about Steve?"

"Haven't seen much of him," Jenny said, hoping Anna wouldn't detect her disappointment.

"Hmm."

"He's been real busy."

"Aren't we all?"

"You know how it is. I can't expect him always to be at my beck and call."

Anna grimaced at the way Jenny was excusing Steve's behavior. "It sounds like you're doing for him what I did for Joe. Be careful."

"I'll try." Jenny swallowed hard, realizing the truth in Anna's words.

Anna looked at her closely and asked, "Are you thinking you might marry him?"

"He hasn't asked me," Jenny said, trying to smile.

"Would you, if he did?"

"I'm not sure."

"Well, take your time to decide, Jenny. Marriage is not an easy road." Anna had always been protective of Jenny in a motherly way. Her sons were off on their own, and her only daughter would have been Jenny's age had she not died suddenly in her infancy. Jenny appreciated the void she filled for Anna. "I never want you to end up in my shoes," Anna said caringly.

Jenny thought the world of Anna and respected her judgment. If Anna could have been so wrong about Joe, how could she do any better with Steve? Her stomach tightened, just like it had with Vance.

Gladys came in with an armful of morning mail. "Got anything there for me?" Anna asked her.

"No, this is all Jenny's. Yours is on your desk."

"I'd better go and take a look. I hope I don't find another interrogatory from Joe's lawyer to fill out."

Jenny reached for a parcel-post package resting on top of a pile of mail Gladys had left. Inside the brown wrapping paper, she found an aqua gift box. She opened the envelope. A check fell out from the folded card. She read the handwritten note: *Don't like ladies buying me lunch, especially when it was so pleasant.* It was signed, *Jack Ross,* and the check he had enclosed more than covered the cost of their lunch at the private club and her hourly fee. *Classy guy,* she said to herself.

She felt carefully through the layers of white tissue paper, then lifted out a lovely hand-painted Battersea enamel box. On its hinged lid was inscribed: *Forget not an old friend. And be choice of a new one.* It was a wise saying, and Jenny smiled at the vivid image she had of Jack Ross, chuckling over his little dig. She, too, appreciated that the saying was contrary to what was practiced daily in Washington, where out-of-favor officials were quickly forgotten.

Jenny looked through her appointment book to see how she might juggle around her already too-tight schedule to fit in some time to meet with Steve's sister. Steve had called to say Kathy was in for a short visit. Jenny didn't want to miss the chance to meet her. They had talked over the phone the day Kathy had arrived. Jenny was too tied up at the time to set a date, and had said she'd try to work something out the following week. But that week was here and already it was as booked as the one before.

The only opening she had was this afternoon. She was having lunch with Sally Mitchell. Jenny had hesitated inviting Kathy earlier. She knew Sally wouldn't mind having Kathy included, but she wasn't certain if Kathy would be intimidated by the prospect of having lunch with a well-known journalist. Looking at her calendar, though, Jenny realized this was the only chance she'd have to get together with Kathy, and she quickly dialed the houseboat, hoping to reach Kathy before she went out for the day. Fortunately, Kathy was home.

"How are things going?" Jenny asked her.

"Pretty good. I've been sort of on my own. Steve's been really busy, but he left me an agenda of what's going on in Washington and what I might like to see. He even arranged for me to have a private tour of the Capitol and the White House. It's just like Hollywood, but instead of actors and actresses, I'm running into senators and congressmen. I've got quite a collection of VIP pictures to show the folks back home." She sounded like a kid who had been to Disneyland, and Jenny realized what good medicine Washington and Steve were for her.

"I know this is short notice, but I'm having lunch with a friend and would love to have you join us, if you're free." Jenny explained to Kathy who that friend was.

"Oh, I enjoy her column. She has such insight," Kathy said.

"Good! So will you come?"

"I'd love to." They planned to meet early so they would have a little time to talk privately before Sally arrived.

* * *

Steve's sister turned out to be the opposite of what Jenny had expected. On reflection, though, Jenny realized that Kathy was exactly what Steve's sister should be. Jenny had arrived early at the restaurant so she could arrange to have the bill charged to her, and she chose a secluded table where she, Kathy, and Sally could talk freely.

Jenny was nibbling on a bread stick while she waited, and an Italian waiter was opening a bottle of mineral water for her when an attractive woman, about Jenny's age, entered the restaurant. She caught Jenny's eye and, Jenny noticed, that of the waiter too. He had stopped pouring the mineral water and was smiling at the pretty sight.

The woman lifted her sunglasses to the top of her head, pushing her dark wavy hair away from her face. The maître d' smiled at her in the same way the waiter had, and pointed in Jenny's direction. Jenny wasn't quite sure if she was Steve's sister. She hadn't expected her to look so stylish. As she walked in Jenny's direction, the tangerine jersey sheath she wore hugged her willowy shape, accentuating the easy, graceful stride that was very much like Steve's. She seemed completely oblivious to heads turning, as Steve would have been.

But when she smiled at Jenny, there was no doubt left as to who she was. Her smile was as warm as Steve's, and her dark eyes just as alive. "Jenny, I'm Kathy, Steve's sister," she said, extending her hand. Her fingers were long, a smaller version of his. Already, Jenny felt good being with Kathy, and she was reminded of how good she felt when she was with Steve.

"I'm sorry I'm late," Kathy said, slipping off her white linen jacket and loosening the yellow and turquoise scarf around her shoulders. "I had trouble finding a place to park."

"You drove?" Jenny asked, surprised that Kathy, being accustomed to country roads, hadn't shied away from Washington's traffic.

"Sure. Steve left me a good street map. I had no problem finding the restaurant." Jenny gathered Kathy wasn't as delicate as she looked.

Jenny filled her in on Sally Mitchell's background. "I told her you would be joining us."

"Did she mind?"

"Not at all." Jenny touched Kathy's hand. "She was just as pleased as I am." Again Jenny wondered if Kathy might not be a little apprehensive about being with two successful women—one she had spoken to only on the phone, and the other a celebrity. But having listened to Kathy speak with such zest, Jenny got the feeling she was the kind of person who enjoyed people, and certainly people couldn't help but enjoy being around her. Kathy seemed to show a "nothing ventured, nothing gained" attitude toward life that comes from being raised in a small town. It was okay if the people in the big city didn't like her. There were folks back home who did. Jenny had known that security once too, but somehow had lost it in Vance's crowd.

Kathy seemed very curious about Jenny's work and asked her all about image making. "We could really use something like that back home," she said. "Things are pretty tough right now. A lot of women are having to go back to work, and farmers are giving up farming." She smiled. "They could use a little help getting out of their work clothes and into a suit!

"Besides, we have a lot of cheap land out there, and I can easily see something happening soon," she said, becoming more excited as she spoke. "Like Silicon Valley in California. Except instead of computers, we could be the center for something like biotechnology. It could work. After all, a lot of biotechnology research is being done to improve livestock and grain. So why not have it done in the Midwest where its primary market is?"

Not only did Kathy share Steve's charisma, but his intelligence too, Jenny thought. "Do you know you and Steve are a lot alike?" she asked.

"People say that. I'm not sure—it's hard to tell. But I'm sure glad he's my brother. I don't know what I'd do without him. He helped me out so much when Chip died. He took care of everything—the funeral, the paperwork, the banks."

Kathy smiled as she remembered. "You should have seen him, coaxing me to drink the malts he concocted. I couldn't eat a thing. And he tried camouflaging anything and everything he could think of inside those malts—eggs, wheat germ, fruit—so I'd get some nourishment. He hardly let me out of his sight. Even at night, if I awoke, I'd find him in a chair by my side. It was as if he was afraid I was going to…." Her voice trailed off. Then she said, "I guess having lost Mary, he knew what it's like."

Yes, Jenny thought, *Steve knows what it's like to lose someone you love. That's why he's putting the farmers' bill ahead of our relationship.* He had known the pain—something she wasn't sure she could bear. Even though Hetty had said Jenny hadn't known love in her days with Vance, and Anna had called her marriage to Joe a lie, Jenny felt she had gotten enough of a taste of love to make her scared. Love took more strength than she felt she could ever have.

Jenny spotted Sally and pointed her out to Kathy. "She looks so little," Kathy said.

"I know. That's the reaction I had too, when

I first saw her. After reading her columns, I had expected her to be a giant."

Sally and Kathy hit it off well, first talking about how living in Washington compared to the country. By the time their pasta was almost finished, their conversation had turned to their husbands.

"It was so good," Sally said, talking about her marriage to David. "But, you know, marriage is work—we spent a lot of time accommodating each other. We really raised each other, helped each other grow. I think modern psychologists call it 'bonding.' "

"Yes, but where does one find the time to bond in this day and age?" Jenny asked, thinking of herself and Steve.

"It's not a matter of time. David and I weren't always together. I had assignments that took me away, and he traveled often to show his paintings at different galleries. It's more a question of attitude than time."

Kathy nodded in agreement. "Do you think you'll marry again?" she asked Sally.

"I really couldn't unless I felt it would be as good as it was with David."

Kathy looked at Jenny. "You know, I'm sure that's how Steve feels too. You're the first one he's seriously dated since Mary. Did you know that?"

"No," Jenny said, her emotions thoroughly in conflict.

"You are. He cares for you very much." Then Kathy asked Sally, "Does the pain of losing your husband ever go away?"

Sally looked her straight in the eye and said, "No." Then she took a deep breath. "When I lost David, I lost my best friend. I could tell him anything. What they say about how time heals is a big lie. I miss him every hour of the day. You just learn to go on."

"How?" Kathy asked softly.

Jenny had already heard enough. She excused herself, saying she had to get back to work. She left the restaurant wishing she could leave everything behind her and return to the time before she met Steve. She could barely handle the little time she had with him, never mind what Kathy and Sally were going through.

Chapter Eleven

Jenny sat next to George's nephew in the front pew of the church, waiting for the wedding ceremony to begin and wondering if Steve would ever arrive. He had called to tell her that he was stuck in a session with some urban congressmen. He hoped to make it to the church, but wasn't sure. "I can't believe there are any farmers in the city," Jenny had said to him.

'There aren't. That's why I'm meeting with them. They've been our toughest opposition."

Jenny wasn't one to shirk off work, having at times been accused of being compulsive in her sense of duty, and was sympathetic to why Steve was so driven. But she was finding the amount of time he was working on the Hill totally unreasonable. There was a limit to things, and it was hard to believe that he couldn't escape for just a few hours to be with her at Hetty's wedding. This was just another disappointment, but a major one, that was whittling down her tolerance.

If he loved her as much as he said, how could he stand being away from her so much? Surely his feelings couldn't be as strong as hers. And she couldn't help but feel she was being used. She was beginning to appreciate the resentment that had built up in Anna through the years.

Lately Anna had confided a great deal in Jenny, revealing her inner feelings and thoughts about her marriage to Joe, and their impending divorce. Jenny had listened compassionately, and couldn't help but see parallels with her relationship with Steve. Anna had put her own needs on hold without complaint while Joe devoted himself to his career. Wasn't Jenny doing the same? Jenny had to admit, though, that there was an essential difference—Joe's motives rose out of a desire for personal advancement whereas Steve's did not. Still, however unselfish Steve's reasons, he had chosen the path he was taking. But she hadn't. And she felt she was being forced to unwillingly sacrifice her time with him for the farmers' cause.

Did loving Steve mean taking up his crusade too? Anna had done that for Joe, spending months alone waiting for Joe to return from his overseas assignments. Just as Jenny passed her nights waiting for Steve to call. Jenny didn't want this kind of life on a long-term basis, nor had Anna.

Forming a consulting firm with Jenny had been Anna's way of seeking relief from the loneliness of Joe's absences. Recently Anna had said that her success might have threatened Joe. That didn't seem to apply to Steve. Jenny's accomplishments didn't appear to threaten him; in fact, he was proud of all she had done. But they weren't married. Would he feel the same if they were? Jenny wasn't certain.

Anna had loved Joe once. Jenny didn't want to end up like her, bitter and disillusioned. After all she'd gone through to rebuild her life after Vance, she felt she owed herself more than that, even if it meant her love for Steve would be unfulfilled.

Jenny looked over at George's nephew, also named George, fidgeting and checking his breast pocket for the wedding ring, as he had already done several times.

The minister came out, and Hetty and George joined him at the altar. Hetty looked elegant and at the same time delicately innocent in her cream silk-shantung suit and lacy white Victorian blouse. A sprig of baby's breath adorned the small spray of pink sweetheart roses George had given her. But instead of wearing it as a corsage, Hetty had delighted George by daringly pinning the flowers in her upswept hair as her bridal garland. A matching rose graced the lapel of George's beige summer suit. Jenny thought that, like the flowers they wore, they made a lovely pair.

The minister opened his book. Jenny took one last look to the back of the church and saw Steve running up the steps. He paused for a second to straighten his tie and smooth back his hair from his flushed face. In spite of everything, she realized she was glad to see him. He blew her a kiss as he entered the pew, and took her hand as they faced the altar.

Then George's nephew shouted, "Stop!" startling all of them. He turned to Steve and asked under his breath, "Do you have a match?" Steve shook his head. "The candles aren't lit," George called out, stumbling out of the pew on his way to the altar. His uncle rolled his eyes. "We should have the candles lit." He excused himself to the minister, and asked his uncle, then Hetty, for a match.

"The candles aren't important," his uncle said, a little annoyed but not angry.

"It would be nice to have them lit," his nephew explained. The minister smiled, one of the most tolerant smiles Jenny had ever seen, and lifted his robe to fish a box of matches out of his pocket. Handing the matches to George, he waited patiently while George lit every candle he could find on the altar. Jenny would have laughed at the spectacle George was making of himself if his love for his uncle and Hetty hadn't been so evident. He wanted everything to be perfect for them.

The wedding bands exchanged, George offered to play a song, his gift for Hetty and his uncle. He left his uncle's side to remove a shiny flute from the oblong case he had left in the pew by Jenny. He gave it a rub with the cuff of his shirt, then wet his lips as he approached the altar. Jenny had never heard anything played with more feeling; the notes pierced through her like Cupid's arrows. She turned to Steve and saw that he was equally moved. When finished, George quietly took his place by Jenny and Steve, his head bowed down. He looked wan, as if he had pushed himself beyond the limits of his talent.

"I've never heard anything so beautiful," Jenny said to him.

He smiled. "I'm glad. I wanted to do something special for my uncle. I could never thank him enough for what he's done for me. If it weren't for him, I wouldn't be playing in the orchestra now. He paid for all my education. He's been like a father to me. My real father took off when I was real little."

Jenny patted his hand in a gesture of compassion. She was glad Steve was with her to share the beauty of his music and the beauty of Hetty and George's love.

They had a good time at the wedding lunch Hetty's new husband hosted at La Coquille, and joked about the monthlong honeymoon George had planned for Hetty. It was the first time Hetty and George had met Steve, and Jenny could tell he was charming them both. Several times, Hetty pulled Jenny aside and whispered in her ear, "Don't you dare let this one get away."

Everyone talked freely, their spirits high, as if they were close family members. Even though George's nephew was so different from Steve, they got along very well, discovering a common bond in their love of classical music—another surprise for Jenny about her country boy. Jenny wondered if she would ever know everything about Steve, especially in light of the little time they had together.

It was midafternoon when they waved good-bye to George and Hetty as their limousine headed for the airport. As they left, Jenny hoped love would be kinder to Hetty than it was to her.

"Do you have to go back to the office?" Jenny asked Steve.

"No, the rest of the day is all ours for a change."

"Is there anything special you'd like to do?"

"How about showing me the music room?" Steve asked, referring to the offer she had made way back on that drizzly, dreary afternoon in March when they unexpectedly met at Dumbarton Oaks. She hadn't been to the gardens since then. It wouldn't have been the same without Steve.

Today the flower beds were a mass of blooms, and the fountains were flowing in full force. Walking back toward the rose garden, she felt herself in a turmoil. So much had happened since they first met. What she had first taken to be a little addition of excitement to her life had become another matter. She wanted to be with Steve and without Steve, all at the same time.

They walked hand in hand for a while, following an out-of-the-way path over terraced walks. They came upon a small pond hidden in the shade of a large weeping willow tree. "This must be Lover's Lane Pond," Jenny said, pleased. "In all the times I've been here, I haven't been able to find it."

He took her chin in his hand. "There's a good reason that it's hard to find," he said. His embrace melted away all her misgivings.

"Oh, Jen," he said. He smoothed her hair and kissed her neck. "I want to be with you day and night," he said as he moved to kiss her lips.

But he wasn't with her day and night, and his saying that only reminded her of it. The memory of all her lonely nights surfaced, freezing her.

"What's wrong?" Steve asked when she withdrew from his arms.

Her buried anger came alive as she thought how little time he had for her lately. "It's hard not being with you," Jenny said, turning from him. "It's hard when you're always putting me on hold on the telephone, canceling dates, and being at Senator Maxwell's beck and call."

"Do you think that doesn't bother me?" He walked around to face her and peered into her eyes. "I don't like it any more than you do."

"But you like getting your bill passed. That's all you care about. You've lost your values."

"My values are still there and stronger than ever," he said. Jenny sensed a controlled but rising anger in his voice. "I'm sorry you've lost sight of them."

"I guess I have."

"You have. Because if I really had lost my values, as you seem to think, I'd forget it all and go back to the farm." He touched her elbow pleadingly, trying to reach her. "You of all people should know the hard work involved in getting legislation through."

"Not when it excludes everything else."

"It has to. I'm here to help the folks back home. They're counting on me. I can't let them down."

"You're letting me down."

"Jen, I'm letting myself down too, when it comes to that. But I'm not free to do what I want until I've accomplished what I came here for."

"So, am I supposed to continue playing second fiddle to Senator Maxwell and all the others?"

He shrugged. "Just a little longer."

A little longer! she said to herself, wondering exactly how important she really was to him. "It's already been long enough," she said, her feelings of rejection boiling over.

"You're acting like the spoiled, high-class girl I once thought you were, rather than the farm girl I know you are," he said, mirroring her anger. She turned away and ran out the garden gates. She stopped a passing cab and jumped in before he could catch up with her.

Chapter Twelve

While talking to Carol McGrath, her shy teenage client, Jenny unconsciously played with the handcrafted medallion around her neck, the one that reminded her of the sun setting over Dumbarton Oaks. It had been a couple of weeks since her blow-up with Steve. Her nerves had fallen apart, and her appetite was failing again, as it had with Vance. Steve hadn't been in touch, and she had only herself to blame for that.

But if he felt one-tenth of the pain she was going through, he would have called. The longer she didn't hear from him, the more convinced she became that she had made a mistake falling in love with him. She couldn't possibly be an important part of his life when he had made it quite clear that he had his work to do and that came first. Well, she had work to do too. Jenny looked at Carol, her anger giving her the energy to go on, and said to herself,

Maybe I can't do anything about my pain, but I sure can do something about yours.

She looked down at the medallion she was fingering and thought she wouldn't be needing the memories it evoked anymore. She lifted it over her head and gave it to Carol. "Go ahead, put it on," she coaxed Carol. *How pretty she is,* Jenny thought, knowing Carol and her mother would find that surprising.

Mrs. McGrath was already a nervous wreck over Carol's coming-out party next year. She had lost sight of Carol's uniqueness and was determined to turn her into a carbon copy of the other girls at her daughter's school, who all looked like models for *Seventeen* magazine.

As Carol put the necklace on, her eyes shone. How could her mother ever have suggested covering Carol's beautiful eyes with blue contact lenses and dyeing her lovely taffy-colored hair a sunshine blond? "There, it's perfect on you," Jenny said. "It's yours."

Carol smiled, and Jenny added, "You have such a lovely smile." She wondered how many times Carol had smiled for her mother.

Keeping up a cheerful front, however, was taxing, and Jenny was exhausted when Carol left. She wished she could unburden herself on Hetty, but Hetty wouldn't be back for another week. And Anna was seldom at her desk, running around like a maniac, refusing to share her load. Jenny knew a lot of it had to do with keeping busy, so she wouldn't have time to think about her pending divorce.

All Jenny had to look forward to was another quiet evening with Amber curled up on her lap. But if she didn't muster up enough willpower to get through the rest of the day, Amber's company was all she would be fit for. She felt like she was walking a fine line, and she would fall into a deep depression if she lost her fight to keep going.

"That creep!" Anna shouted, barging into Jenny's office and slamming the door behind her.

"Who?" Jenny asked, surprised to see Anna in such an angry state.

"Joe, that's who. If you're ready for lunch, I'll tell you all about it."

The minute they were seated at a table in the restaurant, Anna burst out with her news. "I found out who Joe is running around with."

"Who is she?" Jenny asked, disappointed that Joe could do such a thing to Anna.

"Karen Wexley. Have you ever heard of her?" Jenny shook her head. "She's a trade economist with the government."

"How did you find out?"

"A few people let it slip, not realizing I'm Joe's wife. It seems the news is quite widespread. You know how it goes—the wife is the last to know."

"I'd think Joe would have been a little more discreet."

"Oh, I'm sure Mr. Sneak was very discreet. *She* probably let the cat out of the bag, not him. All she had to do was tell one friend. And that friend tells another friend, and before you know it, it might as well be the top story on the evening news."

"Well, this is the first I'm hearing about it."

"That's because you don't work on the Hill," Anna said in a huff, putting her hands on her hips. "I'm sure it's old news there."

"Old? How long has this been going on?"

"Supposedly a while—two to three years, I guess."

"Does she know he's married?"

"Of course. Do you think that would stop her? I'm sure he gave her the usual line about how rotten our marriage is. I wish he had let me in on that little secret."

"Do you know anything about Karen Wexley?" Jenny asked, waving the waiter over to order.

"I questioned Joe about her, and he spilled the beans. From what he said, she must be Miss Personality. That's hard to imagine. Her specialty is potatoes."

"Potatoes?"

Anna nodded. "That's all she does. She's the government's potato expert. Maybe that's why she was attracted to Joe. He's a good couch potato. I've heard from other sources that she's quite a number."

"She runs around?"

"That's right," Anna said, picking up the menu.

"Does Joe know that?"

"Not in the idiotic state he's in. And I'm not going to tell him. He wouldn't believe me, anyway. He'd think it was just sour grapes on my part."

"I guess you're right."

"He's in a hurry to get our divorce settled so he can marry her."

"Why the rush?"

"She's putting pressure on him."

"How old is she?"

Anna squinched her face. "Twenty-eight."

"Twenty-eight!"

"I know. The man's gone crazy. Another May-December marriage. Can you imagine?"

"No, not at all."

"You know," Anna said, once they had ordered, "if our son and his wife decide to have children, Joe would be a grandfather. I can't believe he's dumb enough to get himself into this." Anna took a sip of her wine. Jenny noticed a slight tremor of controlled anger in Anna's hand. "He's so concerned about being fair to her. Well, how about me? Where is his sense of fairness when it comes to me? He talks about monopolizing her youth. Well, how about the nearly thirty years of my life we were married? Are they gone like a puff of smoke?"

It was all inexplicable to Jenny. Anna and Joe had been such a perfect pair. But nothing could be done when Joe inexcusably ignored his responsibilities to Anna and refused any attempt to reconcile or even to hear her out.

"I've given up on saving our marriage," Anna said later, pushing aside the filet of sole she had barely touched. "We're beyond that now—too many things have been said that shouldn't have been. But if only he had agreed to go into counseling with me, then, at least, I might know what happened, what went wrong. That's what hurts so much. If only I could get that one big nagging 'why' answered, maybe it would be easier to accept. But then maybe I'm asking the impossible. You know, when you really get right down to it, I don't even think Joe knows why."

"Maybe it's a monumental mid-life crisis," Jenny suggested.

"I don't know. It seems too simple to pass it off as that. I think it's more a sickness of our times. We just aren't strong enough to handle responsibility and commitment the way our parents did. I know they say a lot about the older generation staying in unhappy marriages. But is what we have now really better? Is one marriage really all that different from another?"

Jenny shrugged her shoulders.

"You want to know something, Jenny? I wish I could say I didn't work hard enough at my marriage. But that wasn't the case. I worked hard, awfully hard. I couldn't have given any more. Yet that wasn't enough to keep it together." She looked closely at Jenny. "Stay single—you're better off. It's just not worth all this trouble."

The restaurant had filled up considerably while they ate. As people were being seated nearer to them, Jenny and Anna talked in more general terms. On their way out Jenny gave an unintentional sideways glance and spotted Steve sitting with Candy Carson at a corner table by the window. He was toasting Candy with a glass of wine. *Well la de da!* Jenny said to herself, clenching her fist. *He's sure not wasting any time!* She hoped she could slip out before he noticed her.

"Jen!" she heard him call out.

She gave him a passing glare but made no effort to respond to his motioning her over to his table. She turned to leave with Anna.

"Is that Steve?" Anna asked.

Jenny nodded and hurried her along. But in barely a second, he had caught up with them.

"The bill passed," he said, looking at Jenny.

The anger in her eyes quickly subdued his excitement. Anna congratulated him with a handshake, then excused herself in a rush to get to an afternoon appointment. Jenny turned to leave too.

Steve grabbed her arm to stop her. "Candy and I were just celebrating. She was on the Hill when the final vote came in. Can't you join us for a minute?"

"I'd rather not interrupt," Jenny said in a biting tone.

"You're not interrupting anything." His uncertainty as to what she might be thinking showed on his face. His eyes searched hers. "Please believe me. Look, I'm sorry about what I said at the gardens. I've missed you terribly."

"But not enough to call."

"I didn't think you wanted me to. Besides, we need to talk, but not over the phone."

"Well, now that the bill is passed, will we have that chance?"

"Yes," Steve said, taking her hand with a smile.

"When? Tonight?"

"There's nothing I'd like better. But Maxwell's throwing a party tonight. This bill is a big feather in his cap."

Jenny paused and stared at him. "And you have to go."

"I should."

"Will Candy be there?"

Steve nodded. "We owe her a lot. We had a lot of help from her in getting that bill through. She sure pulled strings to bring in those industrial votes. Now I have to return the favor and give her my support in getting her legislation passed too. She's one of the many IOU's I need to pay back." Jenny couldn't help but wonder if Candy hadn't aligned herself with Steve for more than political reasons. "You're welcome to come," Steve said, though he didn't sound enthusiastic about her being at the party.

She couldn't figure out why, and coolly said, "No thanks. Will we get to talk soon?"

"Real soon. I've just got a few things to tie up first."

"Sounds like I've heard that before." She felt as if she was being put off. "Call me when you have a free moment," she snapped, and left.

Jenny flicked on the television when she got home that night and curled up in front of it, with a ham and cheese sandwich and Amber by her side. Why had she gotten the feeling Steve didn't want her at the party tonight? Was there something going on between him and Candy? Well, even if there was, she had no rights to him, no ties. And she wished she could break the ties she felt for him. Anna was right. It wasn't worth all this trouble.

The main focus of the evening news was the passage of the farmers' bill and an accompanying review of the struggle that had gone on during the past year to get it through. One of the clippings was of Steve speaking before a Senate panel. He was very impressive, forceful, and totally sincere in his presentation of the farmers' side. *You're all I wanted you to be,* Jenny said to herself, taking a professional point of view. *And you've gone and turned me into a fool.*

Tears of despair ran down her cheeks. Steve had more important things to do than contend with a fretful girlfriend. And that was exactly how she was behaving. She was being selfish in putting demands on him when he already had more than most men could bear. There was no use in continuing to see Steve if she couldn't be strong enough to cope with his tireless dedication to the farmers' interests. The last thing she wanted to do was pull him away from his task, when he was doing so much good.

She bit into her sandwich, then put it back down. It tasted as dry as sawdust. The doorbell rang, and she rose to answer it.

"Steve!" she said, surprised to see him standing there.

"May I come in?" he asked.

"How come you're not at the party with your lady friend?" she said sarcastically.

"Lady friend?"

"Candy."

"Candy? Do you think I'm running around with her?"

Jenny shrugged.

"You've got it all wrong." He seemed worried that she'd even think that.

"Then how come you didn't want me to go to Maxwell's party?"

"I didn't think you'd enjoy being there. It was just a lot of drunks, yelling and screaming." He tried to approach her, but she backed away. "Jen, what's happened to us? I don't want to lose you. I love you too much."

"Love? I can't handle love," Jenny said, falling back onto the couch.

"It's not love. It's your fear of it. Our love really hasn't had a decent chance, not when I've been spending most of my time working on the bill." He sat down beside her and held her hand. "I know it's been hard on you, but it's been even harder on me, because I want to be with you so badly." He took her other hand, as if to bring her more in touch with his emotions. "But my life wasn't my own. I had to get that bill through."

"I know," Jenny said. "I saw the news report tonight on the bill." She didn't want to listen to Steve proclaiming his love when she felt so disappointed in herself. "You came across very well. Now that you've accomplished that, what else do you have up your sleeve?"

"Nothing much. I just plan to stick around and make sure the farmers don't get zapped again."

"The farmers will be glad to hear that," Jenny said, feeling a little more calm. "You're too good a friend for them to lose."

"And you—are you glad?"

She shrugged. "I'm glad you'll be staying in Washington. What you're doing is very important."

"I hope it is. They need someone to watch out for their interests."

"Is that what you're going to do—be a watchdog for the farmer?" she asked, trying to make light of the determination she saw in his eyes and heard in his voice.

He smiled. "I guess so, though I never thought of it that way. But I don't want to just guard them. I want to get things done."

"It sounds like you're considering running for something."

"I've been thinking about it."

Jenny knew he should—honest, upright representatives were hard to find. But that meant she could look forward not only to playing second fiddle to people on the Hill, but to voters too. She'd never see him. Would there ever be a chance for their love? It was hopeless. They should go their separate ways. He should run for office, and she should try to forget him as best she could.

"I'm telling you this," Steve said, "because I want to marry you. I just want you to know what you're getting into." She held her breath, knowing that she could never be the kind of wife he should have. "I know it's not going to be easy, and I'm asking a lot of you. But it's something I have to do," he continued.

"Are you sure?"

"Yes. Just like you have to do what you do. I can't fulfill all your needs."

"But you did that for Mary," Jenny said, though she knew full well that she could never be the stay-at-home wife Mary was. She thrived on the stimulation and challenge her work provided, and she would be lost without it.

"Things were different then. That was before Chip died. Besides, I'm not sure I did fulfill all her needs, or mine. It wasn't perfect."

"What do you mean?" Jenny asked, surprised. If his marriage to Mary wasn't perfect, was there really any hope for them?

"Nothing's perfect, Jen. We can't have it all. Life's a compromise." Then he looked into her eyes and said, "For a long time I've wanted to come to Washington and do what I'm doing. But I didn't think Mary was strong enough to cope with the kind of life I'm asking of you. I think you are."

She looked into his eyes, wishing she were. "I'm not. Look at me—I'm a nervous wreck. I couldn't handle marriage—especially a part-time one."

"Our marriage wouldn't be part-time, not when my love is with you all the time."

"Your love is, but you aren't. The time you've spent on the bill has already given me a taste of what it's like."

"But it would be different if we were married. I'd be coming home to you every night."

"I can't," she said, on the verge of tears. He didn't understand how weak she was, how easily she could crumble.

"You can, Jen. I know your strength." He smiled. "It took strength to escape Vance's control and build a successful career." He bent over to kiss her, but she turned away.

He's better off without me, she thought. "Maybe that's the point—I'm worn out," she said, trying to make him really understand how weak she was. "I don't know if I have the strength left to be your wife."

"Don't you love me enough to try?" he asked, taking her in his arms. She looked down, away from his lips. "Don't hurt me like this," he said.

"I don't want to hurt you." That was exactly why she was refusing him; she didn't want him to be shackled with a crazy wife.

"You are. You're saying you don't love me."

"But I do!" How could he think she didn't?

"If you did, you wouldn't be choosing to say no."

She didn't know how to answer him. He

took his coat hastily. Turning to her as he left, he said, "Love gives no choices, Jen. If you loved me enough, you'd realize that." He closed the door behind him without looking back at her.

She shook her head. If only he understood her fears, he would know how wrong he was about her love for him.

Chapter Thirteen

Jenny's depression deepened during the following month. Anna covered up for her. "I have a mind to call up Steve and tell him to stay out of your life," Anna had said. "If you're getting this upset over him, you're better off without him."

Of course, Jenny forbade Anna to call Steve, and she tried to resign herself to the fact that it was over between them. But the more she tried, the less she could eat. He had said that she didn't love him enough. That wasn't true, but perhaps it was better that he believed it. That was probably why he hadn't been in touch.

She had wanted to call him so many times. But each time her hand shook so badly from nerves that she couldn't even dial the phone. What would she say, anyway? She'd only be repeating that she wasn't sure the kind of marriage he offered her was one she could survive. That she wasn't sure she could cope with the pressures of their dual careers and separations. That would only reconfirm his belief that she didn't love him enough.

Regardless of how much she loved him, he deserved more than a crazy wife. She just didn't mix well with love. It was obvious to her, but not to her heart. No matter how she tried, she couldn't stop loving Steve. She was in such a state that Anna insisted she take a couple of days off and get some rest. She did, but when she went back to work, she didn't feel any better.

Then came the Saturday in August when she was to attend a party given by Mrs. Michel, the ambassador's wife. Jenny woke up that morning feeling the way she had the day before she was to marry Vance. How would she ever manage to attend Mrs. Michel's party that evening? She had tossed and turned all night. Steve had invaded her dreams as he had almost every night. And during the day, she found herself seeing him in the street or in her office, only to blink and realize he really wasn't there.

She felt frazzled, and the junglelike August heat wasn't helping any. Time was not healing, as Anna had said it would; it was only making her think of Steve more and more. Nothing was worth this pain. Why did Steve have to be so committed to a cause? No matter how he had tried to explain it, she didn't want a part-time marriage. Yet now she'd give anything to be with him, if only for five minutes!

Already she could hear the crickets clicking. The blazing sun behind the drawn bedroom shade hurt her eyes, and she turned over. It was going to be another hot and sticky day. It was useless to stay in bed. She got up and looked out the back window. Hetty and George were sitting next to each other under the grape arbor, having their morning coffee.

Watching them reminded her of the couple she had seen the night she had gone out with Steve, when he had told her about Tillie. She and Steve had taken a walk to get some night air, and they had seen a couple eating a bowl of popcorn in front of the TV. She had wished they were inside that house. Just as she now wished that they were sipping coffee in the garden.

Jenny decided to join Hetty and George. She hated to interrupt them, but she needed some company. She couldn't be bothered with dressing, and threw on a cotton robe. She glanced in the mirror as she left her room and ran her hand through her disheveled hair. She noticed the circles under her eyes, but she was too downcast to care.

"Hi, newlyweds," Jenny said to them, trying to sound cheerful.

"Here, sit down," Hetty said, pointing to a chair George had pulled over for Jenny. Hetty poured coffee for Jenny and refilled her own cup. Jenny sensed that their new life together was suiting them very well.

"Would you care for some cream, dear?" George asked Hetty. Suddenly Jenny's mind flashed back again to the night of their first date. After their walk, they had stopped at a cafe for dessert, and Steve had poured cream into her coffee in such a gentlemanly way. She wanted to scream. She felt like she was going to go mad, right then and there.

"Jenny, what's wrong?" Hetty asked.

"Nothing," Jenny said, taking a deep breath, trying to calm herself.

Hetty shook her head and gently said, "You've got to pull yourself together."

"I'm trying," Jenny said, biting her lip, "I'm really trying."

"What you need is a nice stay at my beach house. You won't have to do a thing," George said to Jenny, taking her hand. "The servants care for you. The sun warms you. The trade winds cool you. The palm trees shade you. The ocean soothes you."

Jenny forced a smile at his attempt to cheer her up. Unfortunately, it wasn't working.

"You know, Jenny, it's tough being a man," George went on. "And even tougher being in love with one, especially one who has a cause. You'll never have all of him."

"That's certainly true."

"But isn't a little time together better than none?" George asked.

"That depends."

"Yes, it does," George said. "It depends on the person you love. It's the person that's important, not the time you have together." Jenny noticed Hetty's eyes fixed on George, and she was smiling in agreement with everything he said. "And Steve is quite a guy," George went on, even though Jenny pretended not to listen. "As far as I'm concerned someone who is willing to put what he believes in above his own personal wants and needs comes around about as often as Halley's Comet."

Jenny sighed, thinking, *Don't carry on so, George. I know how special Steve is. But this fragile girl can't cope with someone special. She needs an ordinary guy. She needs someone to eat popcorn with in front of a TV.*

"What someone like Steve deserves is another gem like him to make his life easier," George said. "Heaven knows it's hard enough trying to do some good in this world. He needs someone to watch out for him, care for him, and put him ahead of herself."

"Is that what I'm supposed to do?" Jenny shouted. "And get nothing in return?"

"Jenny," Hetty said softly, "you'll have him in return."

"When? During congressional recesses?" She felt like her head was going to pop off. Why had she come down? She should have stayed in bed.

"If that's your attitude, then forget it, Jenny," Hetty said, shrugging as if nothing more could be done. "You're only thinking of yourself."

George got up to leave for a board meeting at a hospital where he volunteered, and Hetty collected the breakfast dishes. Jenny sat angrily outside in the garden for a few minutes, feeling no one in the world understood her. But Hetty had to—Jenny leaned on her too much.

Jenny found Hetty in the kitchen putting the clean dishes away. "You're wrong," Jenny said. "I'm not thinking about myself." She leaned against the sink by Hetty's side, avoiding her eyes. "It's Steve. He'll end up with a wife nuttier than a fruitcake. I'm not the marrying kind," Jenny added, repeating what she had come to believe.

"That's too bad, because being single sure isn't agreeing with you." Hetty turned from the sink and looked at Jenny. "Without Steve, you're a mess. Face it."

Jenny glanced at her, then looked away.

Hetty took a towel to wipe a plate dry. "Anna means well," she said, "but she's poisoning your mind. There *are* good marriages, Jenny. Where's your courage?"

Tears were too close for Jenny to answer her. She fled up the stairs to her bedroom. "Not the marrying kind" chanted through her mind in her mother's voice. She heard it over and over as she lay on her bed. She couldn't take it anymore.

She dialed home. She had kept in touch and visited her parents, but could never bridge the gap that had formed when she broke off with Vance. Home was the last place she went to with her problems. But she was calling there now.

"I never said you weren't the marrying kind," Jenny's mother said over the phone. "Why would I say that when I don't believe it?"

"But I thought you did when I told you I couldn't marry Vance."

"Others did, but I didn't. I said nothing. Don't you remember?" All Jenny could remember was her father's fury.

"Your father was only thinking of you," her mother said. "He knew you would be well taken care of with Vance."

"But I was so unhappy."

"He could never see any reason for that. When you have to struggle like your dad has to make ends meet, sometimes having enough money can just grow out of proportion. I know it did with him—it became the whole focus of his life. He meant well. He just knew Vance could give you the financial security he never could."

"But I would have died being married to Vance."

"I know. That's why I said nothing. Arguing with your father is impossible. He isn't easy to live with. He has a lot of needs that I have had to meet. It's drained the life out of me. I saw Vance doing the same thing to you. I was glad when you decided to get out. Jenny, I wished I had been as strong as you in my younger days."

"Strong? I'm falling apart." Jenny told her mother about Steve and why she felt she couldn't marry him.

"Jenny, it's not the same as it was with Vance," her mother said. "You were sick when you were with Vance, and you felt better without him. Now you're sick because you're not with Steve. Don't you think your body is trying to tell you what to do? You really have no choice."

She finally realized she didn't. She could never be happy again without Steve.

Chapter Fourteen

Twilight was descending when a cab dropped Jenny off in front of the embassy Mrs. Michel called home. Jenny had almost told the driver to turn around and take her back. She had forced herself to come, pulling a French blue linen dress out of her closet at the last minute. If it weren't for Mrs. Michel, she would have canceled out and stayed home and tried to call Steve.

"Not the marrying kind." Why had Jenny let those words that her mother never said haunt her all these years? How stupid she had been to let her past trap her future. Her mother had helped her to realize the source of her anxieties and doubts, and it had nothing to do with Steve. She wanted him, no matter what, no matter how long. But she had hurt him so and without any cause. Until she knew for sure he still loved her, she felt like she was only a shadow of her doomed self. Steve was the only one who could bring back her joy.

The butler greeted her. She followed him down the hall, unaware of the loud clicking of her heels on the parquet floors, so highly polished that they reflected the bright lights of the Venetian chandeliers. Not even the priceless antiques around her could attract her interest. She was thinking of Steve and how she would tell him she wanted to be his wife. That is, if he wasn't too angry to listen to her.

The butler opened the French doors for her at the rear of a salon, and Jenny stepped outside. The back garden had been transformed into a wonderland. Votive candles twinkled like hundreds of fireflies amid garlands of flowers draped over the edges of umbrella tables. Guests roamed about, some on buffet lines waiting to be served from steaming silver casseroles, others talking by the bar or seated at tables enjoying their food and conversation. At the far end of the walled garden several couples were dancing.

Jenny saw Mrs. Michel wave to her and excuse herself from the group around her. "Oh, I'm so glad you're here," she said warmly, taking Jenny's hand. The wide sleeve of Mrs. Michel's gold and black metallic gown flowed in the air as she raised her arm and pointed toward the garden and asked, "What do you think?"

"It's marvelous," Jenny said, trying to

sound enthusiastic. "You're becoming the toast of the town."

"Thanks to you." Seeing how much Mrs. Michel had come out of her shell was gratifying, and it gave Jenny a lift. Mrs. Michel smiled. "Now I must get back to the others. Go ahead and enjoy the party. You already know some of the people here." She winked, and was off before Jenny could ask whom she was referring to.

Jenny heard the band leader strike up the song George's nephew had played at Hetty's wedding. The male vocalist sang of being afraid to love and thinking love is only for the strong. Jenny felt as if what he said was directed at her. Before the song was finished, she heard a man say, "Hi there."

Jenny turned around. "What are you doing here?" she asked, surprised to see Jack Ross standing by her with a broad smile. "Are you trying to make some land deals?"

He laughed. "If I do, I should give you a cut!" He took the hand Jenny extended and shook it warmly. "I met Mrs. Michel one day coming out of your office. You know, there could be some great real estate opportunities where she comes from. They've got some nice beachfront property. They could use a couple of hotels. Best of all, for the moment, there's no terrorism."

Jenny laughed, shaking her head. "You don't waste a minute, do you?"

"Not a second," he said. "So long now. I'll get back to you later, after I've had a chance to mingle."

Jenny circulated among the crowd. She ran into Chuck Jensen, the speech writer she had sent Steve to, and a few other professional acquaintances and people she knew from Washington's high society. Everyone had endless praise for Mrs. Michel's party. This was by far the best in years. What a flair Mrs. Michel had. How they wished they could do it too. But they agreed that such a sense of style was something one was born with. Jenny smiled, listening and nodding, proud of Mrs. Michel's achievement and the secret part she had played in it.

Jenny went over to the bar to refill her glass of wine. As the bartender handed back her glass, she caught sight of Steve entering the garden. Her heart stopped. His eyes met hers. At first she thought she had seen a smile as brief as a blink of an eye on his face. But it must have been her imagination, for he turned quickly, ignoring her. She was crushed. It was over. She had lost him, and it was all her fault. How could she expect him to love her after all she had said?

She couldn't stand the heartbreak she felt. She wanted to run out, but she was afraid that leaving so early would draw attention to herself. She latched on to Chuck Jensen. He was a good talker, and she could get away with pretending to listen. Once again her well-honed self-composure didn't fail her. But she couldn't control her eyes from wandering in Steve's direction.

Steve looked so tired. She wondered what was wrong. What was it George had said: "A gem to make his life easier"? She was ready to be that. She had gotten to the point where all she cared about was his happiness, not hers. But that realization had come too late.

About half an hour later Jenny noticed some of the guests were beginning to depart, and she decided it would be all right to leave. She excused herself and started looking for Mrs. Michel to say good-bye.

"Hey, Jenny!" she heard Jack Ross call to her. She turned and was shocked to see him leading Steve through the crowd toward her. "I'd like you to meet this guy," Jack said, put ting one hand on Jenny's shoulder and the other on Steve's. "He's just right for you."

Jenny swallowed hard, stammering a little as she spoke. "We've already met."

"Then how come you're not together? A nice-looking couple like you."

Jenny and Steve stared at each other, neither able to speak. She knew Jack was looking from her to Steve as if they were statues. Then he gave Steve a pat on the back. "Looks like you know her a lot better than I thought," he said with a laugh.

"Excuse me," Steve said. "There's someone over there I need to talk to." He left briskly.

"I've got to get back to him," Jack said, his eyes tracking Steve. "He'd know where I can get some cheap farmland."

Jenny was still watching Steve. From the corner of her eye, she saw Jack looking from her to Steve as he had done a second ago.

"Is he the personal problem you were talking about the day we had lunch?" he asked.

She nodded.

"Don't look so worried," he said. "He's crazy about you."

I wish he were, she said to herself. Jack gave her a farewell wave and headed off to talk about land deals with Steve. She stood where she was for a few minutes, too dazed from being so near Steve to move. How stubborn could she have been not to realize that love gives no choices?

Dejected, she didn't bother to find Mrs. Michel. Instead she walked toward a side garden gate where people were exiting. As she reached out for the gate, a hand from behind her pushed it open for her. She turned and saw Steve's face.

"Let's get out of here," he said, taking her hand and leading her away.

Without saying a word, she followed him

down a few blocks into the quiet of the street, then he turned and took her in his arms. He smiled as he bent to kiss her. She was bewildered. He hugged her tight, his strong arms supporting her. All she wanted was to be close to him again.

"Jen," he whispered in her ear, "it's no use. I can't live without you. I'll do anything you want. I'll quit my job. Anything."

"No. Don't do that. The farmers would kill me.

"I've been miserable without you. I've tried to do what Anna said, but I can't anymore."

"Anna?"

Steve nodded. "She told me what was happening to you. She said if I really cared for you, I would stay away from you. I thought she was right when she said you were better off without me. I thought I was fooling myself, thinking you loved me. I just wanted you to be happy."

This all came so suddenly that Jenny could hardly catch her breath. She shook her head. "Anna had it all wrong. She meant well. She really thought she was doing the right thing. I'm afraid what's happened with Joe has clouded her judgment. I know it did mine for a while. But not anymore."

"When I saw you tonight," he said, holding her hand to his face, "I swore I saw love in your eyes."

"You did."

He smiled and kissed her hand.

She smiled back. "I want to marry you," she said. She never saw him look happier.

"What made you change your mind?" he asked.

"My mind had nothing to do with it. I just listened to my heart for a change."

"And what did it say?"

"It said...." She smiled, speaking between gentle kisses she planted on his lips. "'Jenny, you're a fool. You'll always love Steve.'"

A passing couple gave them a disapproving look. "I think I had better take you home," he said, showing her to his car.

Amber jumped onto the kitchen counter as Jenny poured Steve some coffee.

"I think she's hungry," Steve said, stroking the cat's arched back.

Jenny smiled at Amber. "It's not food she's hungry for, it's attention. Hetty and George are at his beach house, and I think she's lonely."

"How about you?"

She took his hand. "Only when you're gone."

"I'm gone a lot."

"I know."

"You sure you can manage that?"

"I'll have to." She was at peace; she had

faced it now. All along, deep down inside, she had known it had to come to this, and it wasn't going to be easy. "I love you too much to have any choice."

"Jen, I love you too. I'll do everything and anything to make this work." He held her and kissed her with the release that comes from acknowledged love. The barriers of doubt, the search for trust were gone. Their commitment had been made; there would be no others. "I love you so much," he whispered. The reasons for her doubts about marrying him no longer existed.

"We must be careful to bond our love," she told Steve as he left.

"What?" Steve asked.

Jenny laughed. "I'll explain tomorrow." She'd tell him about the conversation with his sister, and that she had been thinking Kathy would make a good business partner. After all, opening a branch where he lived would be worth considering. And Kathy with her pioneer spirit would be the one to do it.

She closed her eyes, thinking that every time she and Steve looked at each other, there would be something different, be it another gray hair or a newer cause. There would be no fixed "happily ever after." And for that she was grateful—it would be different from her relationship with Vance. It would be the unknown that would make their life exciting. She pictured herself and Steve in a swirling storm—holding hands and smiling.

Made in the USA
Monee, IL
07 September 2026

62521456R00112